Katie didn't answer. She couldn't. She was too conscious of his nearness, and it brought up all kinds of conflicting emotions within her.

Everything in her told her that this man was some kind of adversary. He was a danger to her peace of mind. And yet when he touched her like this she was instantly lost in a cotton wool world of warmth and comfort.

His arms were around her, his body shielding hers from all that might hurt her, and the searing impact of that tender kiss had ricocheted throughout her whole body. She didn't want to move, or speak. Why couldn't she stay here, locked in his embrace, where the world stood still and she might forget her worries?

Dear Reader

There cannot be many lovelier sights than the glorious sweep of the California coastline where it meets with the deep blue of the Pacific Ocean. I know that's where I longed to be when I wrote my story BECOMING DR BELLINI'S BRIDE.

Even more, I wanted to wander around the vineyards of the Carmel Valley, with their lush fruit hanging off the vines, just waiting to be picked.

This, I decided, was the perfect backdrop for a story of family secrets, yearnings and the desire for the return of land held for generations by the Bellini family.

Of course those cherished dreams bring Nick Bellini into sparking conflict with lovely, idealistic Katie, who is fiercely protective of her father's holdings. Too bad his land once belonged to Nick's family!

And what of the heartache Katie endures when she discovers a long-held family secret…? Will Nick be the one to soothe and comfort her?

I hope you enjoy finding out how everything works out for Nick and Katie.

Joanna Neil

BECOMING
DR BELLINI'S BRIDE

BY
JOANNA NEIL

MILLS
BOON

First published in Great Britain 2011
Harlequin Mills & Boon Limited,
Eton House, 18-24 Paradise Road, Richmond, Surrey TW9 1SR

© Joanna Neil 2011

ISBN: 978 0 263 21887 9

Harlequin Mills & Boon policy is to use papers that are natural, renewable and recyclable products and made from wood grown in sustainable forests. The logging and manufacturing process conform to the legal environmental regulations of the country of origin.

Printed and bound in Great Britain
by CPI Antony Rowe, Chippenham, Wiltshire

When **Joanna Neil** discovered Mills & Boon®, her lifelong addiction to reading crystallised into an exciting new career writing Medical™ Romance. Her characters are probably the outcome of her varied lifestyle, which includes working as a clerk, typist, nurse and infant teacher. She enjoys dressmaking and cooking at her Leicestershire home. Her family includes a husband, son and daughter, an exuberant yellow Labrador and two slightly crazed cockatiels. She currently works with a team of tutors at her local education centre to provide creative writing workshops for people interested in exploring their own writing ambitions.

Recent titles by the same author:

PLAYBOY UNDER THE MISTLETOE
THE SECRET DOCTOR
HAWAIIAN SUNSET, DREAM PROPOSAL
NEW SURGEON AT ASHVALE A&E

CHAPTER ONE

KATIE stood still for a moment, her green eyes slowly scanning the horizon. Her nerves were frayed. Perhaps taking time out to look around her at this part of the sweeping California coastline was just the medicine she needed right now.

She would never have believed she would find herself in such a beautiful place as this small, quiet town, with its charming cottages and quaint shops and general sleepy atmosphere. As for the bay, it was a wide arc of golden sand, backed by rugged cliffs and rocks, a striking contrast to the clear blue of the Pacific Ocean that lapped its shores. Beyond all that was the magnificent range of the Santa Lucia Mountains, lush and green, their slopes forested with redwoods, oaks and pine.

She drank in the view for a moment or two longer, absorbing the tranquillity of her surroundings. Then she pulled in a deep breath and turned away to walk along the road towards a distant building set high on a bluff overlooking the sea.

One way or another, it had been a difficult day so far, and she could see little chance of things improving. She still had to meet with her father, and even though she had become used to seeing him over these last couple of weeks, it was always something of a strain for her to be with him.

'We'll have lunch,' he'd said, as though it was an everyday, natural occurrence.

'Okay.' She'd looked at him and his expression had been relaxed and easygoing. He seemed to genuinely want to meet up with her again. 'I have a half-day on Wednesday,' she told him, 'so that should work out well enough.'

And now he was waiting for her at the restaurant, sitting at a table on the open-air terrace, gazing out over the ocean. Katie guessed he was watching the boats on the horizon. He hadn't noticed her coming towards him, and she was glad of that. It gave her the chance to compose herself, as well as an opportunity to fix his image once more in her mind.

She studied him. He was not as she remembered from all those years ago, neither did he bear any resemblance to the pictures her mother had carefully stored in the photograph album. She guessed at one time he must have been tall and vital, a vigorous man, full of energy and ambition, but at this moment he appeared frail, a shadow of his former self. His body was thin, his face faintly lined, and his brown hair was faded, threaded through with silver strands.

'Hi, there…' Katie hesitated. She was still struggling with the idea of calling this man her dad. It went against the grain to use the word, considering that he was almost a stranger to her. Instead, she asked, 'Have you been waiting long? I'm sorry I'm a bit late. I was held up at work.'

'That's all right. Don't worry about it.' Her father smiled and rose carefully to his feet to pull out a chair for her. 'You look harassed. We can't have that, can we? Sit yourself down and take a minute or two to settle. Life's too short to be getting yourself in a tizzy.'

His breathing was wheezy and laboured, and Katie was concerned. She'd heard that he had been ill for some time, but his health seemed to have taken a downturn even in the few days since she had last seen him.

'Thanks.' She sat down quickly so that he could do the same. Then she gazed around her. 'It's lovely to be able to sit out here and enjoy the fresh air... And it's all so perfect...idyllic, with the tubs of flowers and all the greenery.'

'I thought you'd like it. The food's good, too.'

A waitress approached with menus, and Katie accepted hers with a smile, opening it up to look inside and study the contents. In reality, though, her mind was in a whirl and she was finding it difficult to concentrate, so that the text became a blur.

Her father signalled to the wine waiter and ordered a bottle of Cabernet Sauvignon, before turning back to Katie. 'Why don't you tell me what sort of a day you've had?' he suggested. 'It can't have been too good, by the looks of things. Are you getting on all right at the hospital? You've been there almost a week now, haven't you?'

She nodded. 'I'm really happy to be working there. The people are great...very friendly and helpful. I'm working in Paediatrics most of the time, but I also have a couple of days when I'm on call to deal with general emergencies if they arise locally. Mostly people will ring for an ambulance if there's an accident or medical incident, but if I'm nearer and it's likely to be something serious then I'll go out as a first responder. It's a good opportunity for me to keep up with emergency work, so I was glad with this job came up.'

Her father glanced at his menu. 'It sounds as though it's the kind of work you enjoy. It's what you were doing in England, in Shropshire, isn't it?'

'That's right.'

The wine waiter arrived, pouring a small amount of clear, red wine for her father to taste, before filling two glasses.

Katie took a sip of her drink, savouring the rich, fruity flavour. She sent her father a quick, searching glance. Somehow he always managed to get her to talk about herself. He very rarely revealed anything of his lifestyle, about what had brought him to where he was now.

'What about you?' she asked. 'Did you always have it in mind to come out here—was there something about Carmel Valley that drew you—or was it *someone* who led you to this place?'

'The company I worked for sent me out here, initially,' he answered, placing his menu down on the table. He nodded towards the one she was holding. 'Have you decided what you'd like to eat yet? The filet mignon is always good.'

'Yes, I think I'll go with that. But I'd prefer the cold slices, rather than a steak, I think…with tomato, red onion and blue cheese.'

'And a Caesar salad?'

'That sounds good.'

He nodded. 'I'll grab the waitress's attention.' He studied her once more. 'So what's been happening to get you all flustered today? You've always been calm and collected whenever we've seen one another, up to now. Is it a problem at work?'

She shook her head. 'Not really... I mean, yes, in a way, I suppose.' She gave an inward sigh and braced herself. It didn't look as though he was going to give up on trying to tease it out of her, so she may as well get it off her chest.

'I saw a little boy at the clinic today,' she said. 'He was around four years old, and his mother told me he'd been unwell for some time. She hadn't known what to do because his symptoms were vague, and she put it down to the fact that he'd had a cold and sore throat. Only he took a sudden turn for the worse. When I examined him, his body was swollen with oedema, his blood pressure was high, and his heart was racing.'

Her father frowned. 'Seems that he was in a bad way, poor little chap.'

'Yes, he was. I had him admitted to the renal unit. He was losing protein in his urine, and it looks as though his kidneys are inflamed.'

He winced. 'Definitely bad news. So, what will happen to him now?'

'They'll do tests, and give him supportive treatment. Probably diuretics to bring down the swelling, and he'll be put on a low-sodium, low-protein diet.'

She glanced around once more, looking out over the redwood deck rail to the ocean beyond. The sound of birds calling to one another mingled with the soft whoosh of surf as it dashed against the rocks below.

She looked back at him. 'What about you? You haven't told me much about yourself. Mum said that you worked in the import and export trade years ago—you had to travel a lot, she said.'

'Yes, I did. I suppose that's how I first became interested in the wine business.' He beckoned the waitress and gave their orders. After the girl had left, he said gently, 'This child you treated—he isn't the reason you're not quite yourself, is he? After all, you must have come across that kind of thing many times in the course of your work.'

She nodded, brushing a flyaway tendril of chestnut hair from her cheek. Her hair was long, a mass of unruly natural curls that defied all her attempts to restrain them. 'That's true.' She pressed her lips together, uneasy at having to revisit the source of her discomfort. 'I think he reminded me of a child I treated back in Shropshire… my ex-boyfriend's son, though he was much younger, only two years old. He had the same condition.'

'Ah…' He leaned back in his chair, a thoughtful expression crossing his face. 'So it made you think about the situation back home. I see it now. Your mother told me all about the break-up.'

She sent him a sharp glance. 'You've spoken to my mother?'

'I have.' He gave a faint smile. 'She called me… naturally, when she knew you would be coming out here, she wanted to make sure that you would be all right. A mother's protective instinct at work, I guess.'

Katie frowned, and began to finger her napkin. She wasn't at all pleased with her father knowing everything there was to know about her personal life. In many ways he was an unknown quantity as far as she was concerned, and yet it appeared he knew things about her that she would much rather had remained secret.

She was still trying to take it on board when a man approached their table. He was in his mid-thirties, she guessed, a striking figure of a man with dark, smoulder-ing good looks that sent an immediate frisson of aware-ness to ripple along her spine. His clothes were superb. He was wearing an immaculate dark suit that had been expertly and, no doubt, expensively tailored, while his shirt was made from a beautiful fabric, finished in a deep shade of blue that perfectly matched his eyes.

Those eyes widened as he looked at Katie, and his gaze drifted appreciatively over her, lingering for a while on the burnished chestnut curls that brushed her shoulders, before moving downwards to lightly stroke her softly feminine curves.

Katie shifted uncomfortably in her seat, trying to shake off the impact of that scorching gaze. She felt warm all over, and the breath caught in her throat. Suddenly, she was all too conscious of the closely-fitting blouse she was wearing, a pintucked design in delicate cotton, teamed with a dove-grey, pencil-slim skirt.

Getting herself together, she looked up, deciding to face him head on and return the scrutiny in full mea-sure. He had a perfectly honed physique, long and lean, undoubtedly firm-muscled beneath all the civilised trap-pings. His hair was jet black, strong and crisply styled, cut short as though to tame it, but even so there was an errant kink to the strands. He had the dazzling, sensual good looks of an Italian-American.

His glance met hers and a glint of flame sparked in his blue eyes. Then he dragged his gaze from her and turned to her father.

'Jack,' he said, 'this is a pleasant surprise. It's good to see you.' He extended a lightly bronzed hand in greeting. 'I'd thought of dropping by the house in the next day or so, since you've not been looking too well of late. How are things with you?' His voice was evenly modulated, deep and soothing like a creamy liqueur brandy, and Katie's heart began to thump heavily in response. Why on earth was this man having such an effect on her?

'Things are fine, Nick, thanks.' Her father waved a hand towards Katie. 'You haven't met my daughter, Katie, have you?'

Nick looked startled. 'Your daughter? I had no idea…'

'No. Well…' Her father cut him short, his breath rasping slightly with the effort. 'It's a long story. She came over here from the UK just a fortnight ago.' He switched his attention to Katie. 'Let me introduce you,' he said. 'Katie, this is Nick Bellini. He and his family own the vineyard next to mine. He's in partnership with his father and brother.'

Katie frowned. So her father hadn't even told his friends that he had a daughter. Another small part of her closed down inside. Perhaps she had been hoping for too much. Coming out here might turn out to be the biggest mistake of her life so far.

'I'm pleased to meet you,' Katie murmured. She wasn't expecting him to respond with more than a nod, but he reached for her, taking her hand in his and cupping it between his palms.

'And I'm more than delighted to meet you, Katie,' Nick said, his voice taking on a husky, sensual note. 'I'd no idea Jack was hiding such a treasure.'

Katie felt the heat rise in her cheeks. There was nothing casual about his greeting. The way he was holding her felt very much like a caress and it was thoroughly unsettling. Her alarm system had gone into overdrive

at his touch and it was way more than she could handle.
As if she hadn't had enough problems with men.

As soon as it was polite enough to do so, she carefully extricated her hand. Over the last year she had
worked hard to build up a shield around herself, had
even begun to believe she was immune, and here, in less
than two minutes, Nick Bellini had managed to shoot
her defences to smithereens.

'I've a feeling I've heard the name Bellini somewhere
before,' she murmured. 'In a newspaper article, I think.
I just can't recall exactly what it was that I read.'

He gave her a wry smile. 'Let's hope it was something
good.'

He gave his attention back to her father. 'I was hoping
we could get together some time in the next week or
two to talk about the vineyards. My father has drawn
up some papers, and he'd appreciate it if you would look
them over.'

Her father nodded. 'Yes, he mentioned them to me.'
He waved a hand towards an empty chair. 'Why don't
you join us, Nick...unless you have business to attend
to right now? We've only just ordered.'

Katie's heart gave a disturbing lurch. She stared at
him. What was her father thinking?

'Thank you.' Nick acknowledged the invitation
with a nod. 'I'd like that, if you're quite sure I'm not
intruding?'

He looked to Katie for an answer, but words stuck
in her throat and she had to swallow down the flutter
of uncertainty that rose in her. Why on earth had her
father made the suggestion? They spent so little time
together as it was, and there was so much she wanted to
know, so many questions that still had to be answered.

She needed to be alone with him, at least until she knew him better.

But what choice did she have? To refuse after Nick had shown his willingness to accept the invitation would be churlish.

Of course, Nick Bellini must have known all that. She nodded briefly, but sent him a glance through narrowed eyes.

He pulled out a chair and sat down, a half-smile playing around his mouth. She had the feeling he knew something of what she was going on in her mind, but if he had any real notion of her qualms he was choosing to ignore them.

'I came here to see the management about their wine cellar,' he said. 'After all, we might be able to tempt them into adding our new Pinot Noir to their collection—not strictly my job, but I like to keep in touch with all the restaurateurs hereabouts.' He paused as the waitress came to take his order.

'I'll have the teriyaki chicken, please, Theresa…with a side salad.' He gave the girl a careful, assessing look. 'You've done something different with your hair, haven't you?' His expression was thoughtful. 'It looks good. It suits you.'

'Thank you.' The girl dimpled, her cheeks flushed with warm colour.

Nick watched her as she walked away, and Katie observed him in the process. Did he respond like that to every woman who came his way? Were they all treated to a sample of his megawatt charm?

'Pinot Noir is a notoriously difficult wine to get right,' Jack said. 'But your father seems to have the Midas touch.'

Nick gave a fleeting smile. 'The key is to harvest the grapes in the cool of the evening and in the early morning. Then they're cold soaked before fermentation… and we use the whole berries for that process. Then, to reduce the risk of harsh tannins from the seeds and skins, they're pressed early.'

Jack nodded. 'Like I said, your father knows his business. Your vines are looking good again this year. It looks as though you'll have one of the best seasons yet.' He poured wine into a glass and passed it to Nick.

'We're hoping so.' Nick held the glass to his lips. 'Though you don't do too badly yourself. The Logan name is well respected around here…that's why we'd really like to make it part of the Bellini company.'

'It's a big undertaking.' Jack's features were sombre. 'I've worked hard to build up the business over the years. It's been my life's work.'

'Of course.' Nick tasted the wine, savouring it on his tongue before placing his glass down on the table. 'I'm sure my father will have taken all that into account.'

Katie frowned. It sounded as though the Bellinis were offering to buy out her father's company, but as usual Jack Logan was keeping his cards close to his chest. Was he thinking of selling up, or would he try to fend off their attempt at a takeover?

Nick turned towards Katie, as though remembering his manners. 'I'm sorry to talk shop…I expect this discussion of wine and grapes and company business must be quite boring for you.'

'Not at all.' Katie's expression was sincere. 'In fact I was really intrigued to learn that my father owns a vineyard, and I was actually hoping that one day soon I might get a chance to see it.'

'That won't be a problem,' Jack murmured. 'Just as soon as I get over this latest chest infection I'll take you on a tour. In the meantime, I'm sure Nick would be glad to show you around his place.'

'I'd be more than happy to do that,' Nick agreed, his gaze homing in on her. 'Maybe we could make a date for some time next week?'

'I… Possibly.' Katie was reluctant to commit herself to anything. She wasn't ready for Nick's full-on magnetism. Didn't she have enough to contend with right now, without adding to her troubles? 'I'll have to see how things work out at the hospital.'

'The hospital?'

Nick lifted a dark brow and Jack explained helpfully, 'Katie's a doctor…a paediatrician. She came out here to get a taste of California life and she's just settling into a new job.'

'Oh, I see.'

The waitress arrived with the meals just then, and Katie realised that she was hungry, despite her restless, slightly agitated frame of mind. Perhaps food would help to calm her down.

She tasted the thinly sliced beef. It was cooked to perfection, and the blend of tomatoes and cheese was sublime. She savoured the food, washing it down with a sip of red wine, and for a moment she was lost in a sweet oasis of serenity.

'So what was it that prompted you to come out here just now?' Nick asked. 'I mean, I guess you must have decided to come and see your father, but what made you choose to do it at this particular point in time?'

The peaceful moment was shattered in an instant. 'I… It just seemed to be the optimum moment,' she murmured. 'My contract back in Shropshire was coming to an end...and I'd heard that my father was ill. I wanted to see how he was doing.'

Nick studied her thoughtfully. 'There must have been more to it than that, surely? After all, Jack has suffered from lung problems for a number of years, and yet you haven't been over here to see him before this. Why now? Was it the job at the hospital that encouraged you to make the move?'

Katie frowned. Was that remark a faint dig at her because she hadn't visited her father in the last few years? What business was it of his, and who was he to judge? What did he know of their lives, of the torment she'd been through?

She made an effort to calm down. Perhaps she was being oversensitive...after all, the emotional distance between herself and her father was upsetting. It was a sore point that had festered over the years, and no one could really be expected to understand her inner hurt. And Nick was just like her father, wasn't he, probing into things she would sooner were left alone?

She said cautiously, 'The job was a factor, of course, and I suppose the idea of getting to know more of a different country held a certain appeal.'

Nick frowned. 'You could have taken a longish holiday, but instead you chose to come and live and work here. That must have been quite a big decision.'

Katie shrugged. 'Not necessarily.' She took a sip of her wine.

Jack shifted restlessly in his chair, as though he was impatient with the way the conversation was going. 'The truth is, Nick, Katie had a nasty break-up with a fellow back home in the UK. They'd been together for quite some time. Turns out she discovered he wasn't quite what he seemed, and she learned that he had a child by another woman. Katie still hasn't managed to get over it.'

He speared a piece of steak and held his fork aloft. 'So the long and the short of it is, she finished things with him, upped sticks and headed out here. Of course, he tried to stop her. He pleaded with her to stay with him, but she wasn't having any of it. The child was the one obstacle they couldn't overcome.'

He gave Nick a compelling stare, and Nick's eyes widened a fraction. An odd look of comprehension passed between the two men, as though somehow in that brief moment they had cemented some kind of masculine bond of understanding with one another.

Katie drew in a shocked breath. She felt as though she'd had the wind knocked out of her. Why was her father tittle-tattling her private business, especially to a man she'd only just met? Could things possibly get any worse? She was beginning to feel slightly nauseous.

'Well, that would certainly explain things.' Nick rested his fork on his plate. He studied her curiously, a faintly puzzled but sympathetic expression creasing his brow. 'I'm sorry. I imagine it must have come as a great shock to you,' he murmured. 'These things are very upsetting, of course, especially if it came out of the blue. He obviously meant a great deal to you, this man, if his fall from grace caused you to do something as drastic as to leave home and come out here. That must have been really difficult for you.'

He paused, looking at her, taking in the taut line of her jaw, and when Katie didn't respond, he added gently, 'But he was obviously very fond of you, too, and clearly he tried to explain his actions. I find it incredible that any man would do anything to cause you distress... but, in his defence, people do make mistakes, and I suppose all we can do is talk things through and try to understand how the situation came about.'

He hesitated once more, as though waiting for her to say something, but Katie stayed mute. She couldn't speak. Inside, she was a cauldron of seething emotions.

Perhaps her continuing silence had thrown him off balance because he added cautiously, 'It's not necessarily such a bad thing, fathering a child out of the confines of marriage...these things do happen sometimes. It's how people deal with the aftermath that probably matters most—they have to accept responsibility for their actions, and then perhaps we all need to take on board what's happened and move on.'

Katie took a deep breath and finally found her voice. 'So you've studied psychology along with wine production, have you, Mr Bellini?' Her gaze was frosty. 'I do appreciate you trying to help—I'm sure your theory has a good deal of merit, but, you know, I think I handled the situation the very best way I could.'

She stabbed at a slice of green pepper on her plate. 'Since I'd been with my fiancé for some three and a half years and, bearing in mind that his child was just two years old, I wasn't about to deal with his fall from grace lightly. I'm pretty sure we talked it through to the nth degree, and I have a very good idea of how the situation came about. I'm also in no doubt that James accepted full responsibility for his actions. For my part, I acknowledged totally what had happened...and I decided to move on.' Her green glance locked with his. 'That's one of the reasons why I'm here now.'

Nick looked as though he'd been knocked for six. 'It never occurred to me that any man would cheat on you,' he said in a preoccupied tone. 'I'd assumed the child was born before you met.' He held up his hands in a gesture of capitulation. 'Okay… I admit defeat. I was totally out of order. Clearly, it's none of my business and I was wrong to try to intervene.' He frowned. 'And you must call me Nick. I insist.'

Katie gave a crooked semblance of a smile. 'Perhaps it would be for the best if we change the subject?' She glanced at her father. He had started all this, but he seemed altogether indifferent to the havoc he had caused. He simply picked up the wine bottle and began to refill her glass.

'This is an excellent vintage,' he said. 'I'll order another bottle.'

Katie took a sip of wine. 'Tell me more about the vineyards,' she said, shooting a glance towards Nick. 'How much involvement do you have, if you're in partnership with your father and brother? Do you each have separate roles?'

'We do. I deal with the wine-making process rather than the growing side of things, whereas your father is more interested in aspects of cultivation. It's intensely important to get it right, if we're to produce a select variety of wines. You must let me show you the winery—I'm sure you would enjoy a visit. Maybe you could come along for a wine-tasting session?'

'Maybe.' She wasn't about to agree to anything.

'I'll give you a call some time and see if we can arrange a date.' Clearly, he wasn't about to give up, but by now Katie was well and truly on her guard.

From then on, they kept the conversation light. The

meal progressed, and Katie tried to damp down her feelings of antagonism towards this man who had cut in on her time with her father. What did her father care about her sensibilities, anyway? Perhaps she was wasting her time trying to find out why he had left all those long years ago.

And as to Nick Bellini, she had made up her mind that she would steer clear of him...no matter how hard he tried to persuade her into another meeting. He had touched a nerve with his comments, leaving her unusually rattled, and, besides, she knew it was a matter of self-preservation to avoid him. He could turn on the charm as easily as igniting a flame. She had been burned once. She wasn't going to risk body and soul all over again.

CHAPTER TWO

'No, Mum, I really don't want to go and live with my father.' Katie frowned at the idea. 'He suggested it but, to be honest, it would be like living with a stranger. After all, we barely know one another...even after three weeks I still haven't really managed to fathom him out.'

She glanced around the medical office that she had begun to call her own and leaned back in her seat, beginning to relax. There were still some ten minutes of her coffee break left, more than enough time to sit and chat with her mother.

'These things take time, I suppose...' her mother said, 'but I think it was a wise decision to go over to California to see him. You would never have been comfortable with yourself if you hadn't gone to seek him out. I suppose we all need to discover our roots, if only to find out if there are some genetic characteristics that have been passed on.' Her tone was pensive. 'I know you're like your father in some ways—you know what you want, and once you've made up your mind, you go after it. That's why you've done so well with your medical training.'

Eve Logan was thoughtful for a moment or two, and Katie could imagine her at the other end of the line, mulling things over. 'It's a shame you couldn't find a place to stay that was nearer to the hospital, though,' Eve added. 'A half-hour drive to work every day doesn't sound too good, though I expect it could have been worse.' She hesitated. 'Anyway, how is your father? From what you said last week, it sounds as though he's more ill than we suspected.'

'He has breathing problems—he's suffering from what they call chronic obstructive pulmonary disease.' Katie had spoken to her father about his difficulties, and though he'd been reluctant to dwell on his problems, he'd at least opened up enough to give her a brief outline. 'He's taking a variety of medicines to keep it under control, but I don't think they're having the desired effect. I suspect his condition's deteriorating. He puts on a show of being able to cope, but I can see that it's a struggle for him sometimes.'

She paused. 'Anyway, you're right, it makes me even more glad that I decided to come out here when I did. No matter what I think about him, he's my father, and I feel as though I have to get to know him. Trouble is, every time we meet, he manages to sidestep my questions one way or another, or we're interrupted somehow.'

It still rankled that Nick Bellini had come along to disrupt her lunch with her father, though in truth she couldn't really blame him for that. He was an innocent bystander in all this, wasn't he, and how could he know what kind of relationship they had?

Still, he'd reached her in more ways than she could have imagined. Her father's business associate wasn't someone she would easily forget.

'That must be annoying,' her mother acknowledged. 'Still, you have plenty of time to build up some kind of relationship with him. You've signed a contract for a year, haven't you, so you don't have to rush things... and if, in the end, it doesn't work out, you can always come home. There'll always be a place here for you.'

'Thanks, Mum. That's good to know.' Katie's mouth made a rueful curve. She made it sound so easy, but the truth was, her mother was making a new life for herself back in Shropshire. She was going to marry Simon, a director of the pharmaceutical company where she worked, and they were very much wrapped up in one another right now. Katie wasn't going to do anything to intrude on that.

'Anyway,' she said, 'in the meantime, the scenery around here is fantastic, and with any luck I'll get to see the vineyard before too long. It's not as big as the Bellini vineyard next to it, but by all accounts it's quite impressive.'

'Bellini—I've heard that name,' her mother commented, an inflection of interest in her voice. 'There was an article about them in the Sunday supplement some time ago...all about the different varieties of wine they produce, as I recall. Apparently their land included your father's vineyard at one time—there was something about an Italian migrant seeing the potential for development at the turn of the last century and buying up as much acreage as he could afford. But as the generations went by there were financial problems and part of the land was sold off around 1980. As far as I know, your father didn't get into the business until some twenty or so years ago.'

'Well, he's made a success of it, by all accounts,' Katie murmured. Her mother's comments about the Sunday supplements had triggered a thought process in her mind, but she still couldn't remember what it was that she'd read about Nick Bellini. Some kind of high-society gossip that kept the Sunday papers occupied for a week or two, but annoyingly the gist of it had slipped her mind.

Her pager began to bleep, and she glanced at the small screen, quickly scanning the text message from her boss. 'I'm sorry, Mum,' she said, 'but I'll have to ring you back later. I have to go out on an emergency call. Someone's had a fall at a hotel nearby, and I need to go and see what the damage is.'

'All right, Katie, love. Take care of yourself. Remember I'm always here for you.'

'I will. Bye, Mum.'

Katie grabbed her medical bag and stopped by the reception desk on her way out. 'Divert any patients to Mike O'Brien, will you, Carla? I'm going out on a call to the Pine Vale Hotel.'

'I'll do that. No problem. You'll find the hotel just off the main road out of here.' The clerk gave her a wave as Katie disappeared through the wide front doors of the building.

Pine Vale Hotel was up in the hills, only a short drive from the hospital, and Katie reached it in good time. As she slid out of her car and took a look around, she was stunned by the magnificence of the building. White painted, it was a long, symmetrical edifice with two front extending wings at either end. It stood three storeys high, and there were large, Georgian-styled windows in abundance, with green painted shutters folded back. On the ground floor several sets of French doors were set back in archways, and Katie guessed the hotel must be flooded with light.

She wasn't wrong. Inside, the foyer reflected a quiet elegance, with traditional, comfy sofas that invited people to sit and take their ease. There were low, marble-topped tables and flower arrangements everywhere, adding glorious splashes of colour to delight the eye.

'Hello.' Katie introduced herself to the woman behind the desk. 'I'm Dr Logan. I understand you have a patient for me.'

'Oh, thank goodness you're here.' The woman, around thirty years old, with fair hair cut into a neat, gently curving bob, looked relieved. 'Yes, please come with me and I'll take you to her. The ambulance is on its way...the emergency services said they were sending a doctor out as well, as there might be a head injury, so I'm really glad to see you. I'm Jenny, by the way... Jenny Goldblum. I'm the hotel manager.'

Katie nodded acknowledgement. 'I was told that the lady fell in her room and appears to be semi-conscious—did anyone see the fall? It always helps to know the circumstances.'

Jenny shook her head. She pressed the button for the lift, and frowned as the door swished open. 'It isn't clear what happened. The maid found her when she went to clean the room. We think perhaps it had only just hap-pened because a lady in the room next door had been speaking to Mrs Wyatt just a minute or so before.'

They stepped out of the lift on to the first floor, and Katie was ushered into a large, airy room, furnished in elegant style. There was a double bed with bedside units and an oak dresser to one side of the room, but at the far end, by the window, furniture had been arranged in a seating area. There was an oval oak coffee table and a couple of brocade-covered straight-backed chairs, along with armchairs upholstered in a matching fabric.

The patient, a woman in her fifties, was lying on the floor by the dresser. 'What's her first name?' Katie asked. 'Do you know?'

'It's Laura,' Jenny answered. 'She's staying here with her husband, but he went out earlier for a walk. We haven't been able to contact him yet.'

'Okay, thanks.'

The woman was being tended by one of the hotel staff members, but the girl moved aside as Katie approached. A rug covered the area close by, and it looked as though this had been crumpled when Mrs Wyatt fell.

Katie went to kneel down beside the injured woman. 'Mrs Wyatt...Laura...I'm Dr Logan. Can you hear me? Are you able to answer me?'

Laura Wyatt mumbled something indistinct and Katie tried again. 'Do you feel pain anywhere, Laura?' she asked gently. 'Can you tell me where it hurts?'

Again there was a muffled reply, and Katie came to the conclusion that Mrs Wyatt was too dazed to answer properly. She began a swift initial examination, checking for any obvious injuries and finishing with a neurological check.

'Laura,' she said at last, 'I think you've broken your shoulder—I know that it must be very painful, so I'm going to give you an injection to help with that. Do you understand what I'm saying?'

Laura tried to speak, but whatever she was trying to say didn't come out right, and Katie went ahead and set up an intravenous line. 'We're going to get you to hospital just as soon as possible,' she told the woman. 'In the meantime, I'm going to try to make you more comfortable with a sling that will stop you moving your arm.'

It wasn't clear whether Laura understood or simply couldn't answer, but Katie went on with her examination, checking her patient's blood pressure and listening to her heart.

'What's happened here?' A familiar male voice disturbed Katie's quiet concentration, and she looked up to see with a shock that Nick Bellini had entered the room. 'Katie?' He frowned, studying her for a moment, then turned his attention to her patient. Mrs Wyatt was groaning faintly.

His expression became grim, his eyes an intense, troubled blue.

'Nick?' Katie queried, removing the stethoscope from her ears. What was he doing here? And why had he thought it would be all right to come barging in that way? 'You really shouldn't be in here,' she told him. 'I'm examining a patient.'

'Yes... I see that. I'm sorry for intruding, but you have to understand, I own this hotel... I came as soon as I heard... I'm very concerned that someone has been injured on the premises.' His glance went to the woman once more. 'How is she?'

Katie's eyes widened. He owned this beautiful place? Was there no end to the extent of his empire? She blinked, and then hurriedly dragged her mind back to the business in hand. 'She has a fractured shoulder. I'm sure you must be very worried,' she murmured. 'That's understandable...but this lady has a right to privacy. I think you should leave.'

His head went back, a lock of midnight hair falling across his brow. He seemed stunned by her words, as though it hadn't for an instant occurred to him that anyone would ever try to evict him from where he wanted to be. She waited, bracing herself and expecting an argument, but then he said briefly, 'You'll keep me informed?'

Katie nodded, and without another word he turned and strode out of the room.

She went back to treating her patient. Nick's intrusion had set her emotions in turmoil once more. She had thought she had seen the last of him, and yet here he had turned up when she'd least expected him. His presence had thrown her completely off balance, and now, perhaps because she'd just learned of his association with the hotel, there was a snippet of a newspaper headline running through her head... Something about an heiress...the daughter of a hotel magnate... and Nick Bellini.

She made an effort to push all thoughts of him to one side, and concentrated her attention on her patient, helping the woman to sit up. Then she put the immobiliser sling in place.

'That should keep you fairly pain free until they can take care of you at the hospital,' she said.

The paramedics arrived a few minutes later, and Katie went with them to oversee her patient's transfer to the ambulance. By this time Laura's husband had arrived, and he went along with her, sitting beside his wife and holding her hand.

Katie turned to go back into the hotel, only to find that Nick was right there by her side. She gave a startled jump. He seemed to tower over her, his body firm as a rock. She took a moment to gather herself together and then she gave him a fleeting once-over. He was turned out as faultlessly as ever, dressed in a perfectly tailored dark suit that made him every inch the businessman, a force to be reckoned with.

He looked at her. 'A fractured shoulder, you said. Was she able to tell you what caused her to fall? Was it possible that it could have been the rug in her room—might she have tripped?'

She frowned, walking back with him into the foyer of the hotel. 'Are you worried about liability?' she asked. 'Is that why you rushed over here?'

'First and foremost, I came to see how the lady was doing…but, yes, I have to think about the hotel's liability in this. We take every precaution, but if someone were to be hurt on the premises, it could lead to some very worrying consequences.'

'Well, unfortunately I can't really say what caused the accident. Mrs Wyatt was too dazed to give me any answers, I'm afraid. All I know is that she'll probably need to have shoulder replacement surgery—she fell heavily and it was a nasty injury.'

His mouth flattened as he absorbed that information. Then he said in an even tone, 'Do you have to rush on to another call, or would you have time to stay and have a drink with me?'

She hesitated. Part of her wanted to walk away and avoid getting involved with him any further than need be, but another bit of her recognised his concern. He was anxious for the woman's well-being, and as a hotel proprietor he must be all too conscious of the threat of litigation. Maybe it wouldn't hurt to stay for a while and talk things through with him.

'I don't have to be back at work—my surgery hours are finished for the day, but I'm still on call, so perhaps we should make it coffee rather than anything alcoholic?'

He smiled, his face relaxing for the first time, reminding her all too potently of that sizzling allure that had made her go weak at the knees the first time she'd met him. She had to keep a firm hold on herself. This man could annihilate her sense of security with just one look, and that wouldn't do at all. She'd been down that road, and from her experience it led to heartache…big time. Emotionally, James, her ex, had scarred her for life. She'd been blissfully unaware that he'd been cheating on her, and once his indiscretions had come to light it had torn the heart out of her.

'We'll go out on to the sun terrace,' he said. 'I'll have Jenny send us out a tray of coffee. Just give me a moment to catch up with her.' He lightly cupped Katie's elbow, as though to keep her close, and she stood still for a moment while he beckoned to Jenny. That light touch was like a searing brand on her soft flesh.

The hotel manager was waiting by the desk, talking to the receptionist, but she turned and came over immediately.

'Ask chef to make up a lunch tray, will you, Jenny? Dr Logan will be staying for a while. We'll be out on the terrace by the shrubbery.'

Jenny nodded. 'I'll do that.' She glanced at Katie. 'Is Mrs Wyatt going to be all right?'

'I hope so,' Katie answered. 'The shoulder will give her some problems for quite a while, but those can be dealt with. I'm more concerned about her lack of response. They'll have to do tests at the hospital.'

Jenny nodded and hurried away to find the chef. Nick ushered Katie across the foyer and lounge then out through wide glass doors onto a paved area that was set out with white-painted wrought-iron tables and chairs. The scent of roses filled the air, and Katie was struck by the mass of colour all around, shades of crimson, yellow and pink shrub roses, all vying for attention in the landscaped garden.

'It's really beautiful out here,' Katie murmured as they sat down at one of the tables. 'Everything I've seen so far is overwhelmingly luxurious. I had no idea that you had other interests aside from the vineyard.'

He smiled. 'This place has been in my family's possession for many years—as far back as I can remember. I took it over when my father decided it was time to cut back on his commitments. I bought him out, rather than see it fall to outsiders.'

She gave him a considering look. 'The family name means a lot to you, doesn't it? You're very conscious of your heritage.'

He nodded. 'That's true. Generations of my family have lived in the valley since the end of the nineteenth century, and my great-great-grandfather worked immensely hard to make a go of his enterprise. I feel that we have a duty to secure the results of his labour for generations to come.'

Two waitresses came out on to the terrace just then and placed laden trays down on the table. On one there was a porcelain coffee pot, along with cups and saucers, cream and sugar. The other held an appetising selection of food, as well as plates and cutlery.

Nick began to pour coffee for both of them. 'It isn't just about my own heritage. At the same time I believe we have to give of our best to the local community. That's why what happened this morning concerns me so much. We hold a certain position of trust out here. People look to us to set standards.'

He offered her a plate and napkin. 'Please, help yourself to food.'

'Thank you. It looks delicious.' She gazed at the tempting choices before her. There was *prosciutto*, a dry-cured Italian ham, cut in paper-thin slices, along with sun-dried tomatoes, gnocchi and a crisp salad.

She added a little of each to her plate. 'I wish I could be of more help,' she said quietly, 'but until Mrs Wyatt recovers enough to tell us what happened, we can only wait for the test results to come back from the hospital and hope that they will give us some clue.'

'Was there any head injury?'

'Not that I could see. Of course, that doesn't always mean there's nothing to be concerned about. Any kind of extreme jolting movement within the skull can cause problems that might develop later.'

He tasted a portion of the ham. 'I'll go and see her just as soon as the doctors have had time to treat her shoulder. In the interim I've sent the under-manager along to the hospital to see if we can do anything to make her stay more comfortable.' He frowned. 'It's a dilemma. We generally make sure that the rugs in the rooms are in good condition, not easily rucked. If it was the case that she tripped, I'll have to think about having them removed.'

Katie glanced at him across the table. His concern seemed genuine, and she wondered if there was any comfort she could offer.

'It's always possible that she might have a health problem that caused her to fall—something quite unrelated to the hotel. She might have suffered a dizzy spell, for instance.'

'Or a TIA, perhaps.'

Transient ischaemic attack… Katie gave him a considering look, and slid her fork into succulent, sauce-covered potato gnocchi, giving herself time to think. 'That's a definite possibility. Any restriction of the blood supply to the brain could cause a temporary loss of consciousness.'

'Or stroke-like symptoms.'

She nodded. 'It sounds as though you have some experience of the condition. Has someone in your family had problems with TIAs?'

'No, nothing like that.' His gaze meshed with hers. 'As it happens, I'm a doctor, like yourself. I suppose that's why I didn't think twice about rushing in on you when you were examining Mrs Wyatt. I'm so used to tending these medical emergencies that it didn't cross my mind to steer clear.'

She gave a soft gasp. 'I had no idea.' She studied him afresh, a small frown indenting her brow. 'I can't imagine how you find time to practise medicine when you have a vineyard and a hotel to run.'

He laughed. 'I guess it would be difficult if I tried to do all three…but the fact is, I have managers to do the day to day work for me. They let me know if any problems arise that need my attention—like today, for instance. Jenny called me. Otherwise, I make regular checks to make sure that everything's going smoothly, but for the most part I work in the emergency department at the hospital.'

Her eyes widened. 'That must take some dedication. After all, you could have chosen to stay in the valley and reap the benefits of years of grape cultivation. Your wines are internationally famous, according to my mother.'

'That's true. But I've always wanted to be an emergency physician. When I was a teenager, I saw one of my friends injured in a traffic accident. It was horrific... and for a while it was touch and go as to whether he would survive. Thankfully, he had the best surgical team looking after him, and he made it in the end. It left a huge impression on me. So, you see, I'm passionate about my work, and I can't think of anything else I'd rather do. After all, saving lives is a job that's definitely worthwhile. It gives me more satisfaction than I could ever get from gathering in the grape harvest.'

'I can see how you would feel that way but, then, I'm biased.' She gave a faint smile. 'I have to admit, though, there are times when I'm tempted to swap it all for the kind of life I see out here...lazy days in the sunshine, a trip down to the beach to watch the surfers ride the waves...but then I come back to reality. I couldn't give up medicine. It's part of me.'

He nodded, his glance trailing over her. 'I was surprised to see you here. I remember you said you were a paediatrician...but you did a pretty good job of taking care of Mrs Wyatt, as far as I could see. She didn't appear to be in any pain, there was an IV line already in place, and you had her on oxygen. No one could complain at the standard of treatment she received.'

'Let's hope not, anyway.' She guessed he was still thinking about the repercussions of that morning's accident, and how it might affect him as a proprietor. 'I do work as a paediatrician most of the time, but I'm on call two days a week. During my training, I specialised in both paediatrics and emergency, and I wanted to keep up my skills in both those fields. This job was ideal.'

'I can imagine it would be.' He smiled, his gaze slanting over her, and then he waved a hand towards a platter. 'Won't you try our Burrata cheese? I think you'll find it's out of this world.'

'Thanks.' She helped herself to one of the cheeses, a ball wrapped in mozzarella, giving it a springy, soft texture. As she bit into it, she savoured the buttery texture of the centre, a mixture of cream and shredded mozzarella. 'Mmm,' she murmured. 'It's like a little taste of heaven.'

He chuckled, his gaze moving over her, flame glimmering in the depths of his blue eyes. 'Your expression said it all.' His glance slid to the soft fullness of her mouth and lingered there. 'What I wouldn't give to have savoured that with you,' he said on a husky note. 'You have the lips of an angel…soft, ripe and exquisitely sensual.'

She stared at him, her green eyes widening in confusion. His words took her breath away, and a tide of heat rushed through her body. 'I… Uh…' She didn't know what to say to him. She wasn't prepared for his reaction and his comment was unexpected, disarming, leaving her completely at a loss.

Nervously, she swallowed the rest of her coffee then ran the tip of her tongue over her lips, an involuntary action to make herself feel more secure, to help her to know that all was as it should be, and he made a muffled groan.

'Don't…please…' he said, his tone roughened, his gaze darkening to reflect the deep blue of the ocean. 'That just adds to the torment.'

Katie's pulse began to thump erratically, and a torrent of heat rushed to her head. Panic began to set in. Why was he having this strange effect on her? Hadn't she come all the way out here to start afresh? She didn't want any entanglements, and yet Nick seemed to be constantly in her face, a powerful, authoritative man, someone it was hard to ignore. He wasn't like other men she had met, and she was finding she couldn't trust her instincts around him. At the first foray into dangerous territory she was conscious of the ground sliding out from under her feet. She couldn't let him do this to her.

She straightened, leaning back in her chair. 'Perhaps I should leave,' she said distractedly, her thoughts spiralling out of control. He was altogether too masculine, too hot-blooded for a girl like her. With just a word, a touch he had her senses firing on overdrive.

'Surely not?' he murmured. 'Please, stay a while longer.'

She shook her head. Her bewildered mind searched for options, rocketed from one impossible scenario to the next and collapsed in a panicked heap. 'I've probably spent way too much time here already,' she managed. 'It was good of you to offer me lunch. Thank you for that, but I should be on my way now.'

He reached out to her, laying a hand over hers when she would have drawn back from the table. 'Don't let me frighten you away, Katie. It's just that you shook me to the core the first time I met you, and that feeling hasn't gone away. You're really something special and I'd do anything to see you again.'

She gently pulled her hand out from under his. 'I'm sorry... It's not that I have anything against you, Nick, but I'm not in the market for relationships right now. I just... There are too many things going on in my life, too many changes I have to deal with.'

It was all too much for her. The business with James had hurt her deeply, made her guarded and uncertain, and now she was struggling to build a new life, trying to find her niche in a new job. She couldn't deal with any distractions right now, and she sensed that Nick was way more trouble than she could ever handle.

She pulled in a deep breath and stood up, pushing back her chair. 'Thanks again for lunch,' she said, hating herself for the slight tremor in her voice. 'It was delicious...but I really must go.'

He wasn't going to make it easy for her, though, she discovered. He came to stand beside her, his body so close to hers that she could feel the heat coming from him, could register the heavy thud of his heartbeat as he leaned towards her and slid an arm around her waist. Or was that her own heart that she could feel—that pounding, intense rhythm that warned of imminent danger? His hand splayed out over her rib cage, and her whole body fired up in response.

'That's such a shame,' he murmured. 'There is so much more I want to say to you. I could even show you around the hotel if only you would stay a little longer.'

She shook her head, steeling herself to resist the lure of his embrace. She couldn't allow herself to lean into the warmth of his long, hard body, no matter how great the temptation. 'I can't,' she murmured. 'I... I really ought to go back to the office and type up my notes while everything's fresh in my mind.' It sounded such a weak excuse, even to her ears.

'Such mundane tasks, when life could be so much

more interesting.' He sighed, reluctantly giving in. 'If you're determined to go, you must at least let me walk you to your car.'

She nodded. 'Okay.' At least he was yielding to her decision. Escape was within reach at last, and maybe soon the fog of indecision would lift from her mind... though it didn't help at all that he kept his arm around her as they headed back through the hotel.

Only when they reached her car did he let her go and finally she began to breathe a little more easily.

'I imagine you have to write up a report on Mrs Wyatt's accident,' he said on an even note, 'for the inquiry.'

'Yes.' She nodded. 'There'll more than likely be an official investigation. I gather any kind of accident on public premises causes the wheels to be set in motion.'

'Hmm...do you have any idea what will go in your report?'

She sent him a quick glance. 'I can only state the facts. Anything else would be pure conjecture.'

He considered that for a moment, a line indenting his brow. 'Yes, of course.' He pulled open the car door for her and held it while she slid into the driver's seat. 'I'd be interested in hearing the results of the tests.' He paused. 'Anyway, I expect we'll run into one another again before too long.

She nodded. 'I should think so.' He closed the door and she turned the key in the ignition, starting up the engine.

She frowned as an errant thought dropped into her mind. He'd asked about the report and what she might put in it...and for a good deal of the time while they had been eating he had been asking about the precise details of Mrs Wyatt's medical condition.

Was he worried about the outcome of the investigation and how it would affect the hotel?

Her report could sway things one way or the other. Was that the real reason he was making a play for her? Why would a man such as him be interested in her, after all, when no doubt he could take his pick of beautiful women? The thought disturbed her. She had to tread cautiously, and she couldn't take anything or anyone at face value these days, least of all Nick Bellini.

CHAPTER THREE

'I'M SURE I'd have been all right if we'd stayed at home,' Jack Logan said. His breath was wheezy, coming in short bursts, so that Katie frowned. 'There was no need for you to bring me to the hospital,' he added, struggling to gulp in air as he spoke. 'It's your day off. You shouldn't be tending to me.'

'You're ill,' she said firmly. 'And I'm your daughter, so of course I should be looking after you.' He was a proud man, not one to ask for help, and up to now she had been cautious about stepping in where she might not be wanted. Today, though, he had reached a point where medical intervention was imperative. 'You need to see a doctor right away so that we can get your medication sorted out. You can't go on like this. I won't let you.'

He didn't answer and she suspected his strength was failing fast. She wrapped an arm around him, supporting him as she led him to a chair in the waiting room. The emergency department was busy at this time of the day, just after lunchtime, but she hoped they wouldn't have too long to wait. Her father's breathing was becoming worse by the minute, and it was worrying her.

She paused awkwardly, scanning his features.

'You have your tablets with you, don't you…and your inhaler?'

'Yes.' He eased himself down on to the padded seat, dragging in a few difficult breaths and giving himself a minute or two to recover.

'Perhaps you should have a few puffs on the inhaler now. It might help a bit.' She watched as he fumbled in his pocket for the medication. 'Will you be all right for a minute or two while I go and have a word with the clerk on duty?'

He nodded. 'I'll be fine. I don't need to be here.'

She made a wry face and turned to walk over to the reception desk. He was stubborn and independent, but she wasn't going to let him get away with trying to bamboozle her. He was in a bad way, and he needed help…maybe even to be admitted to hospital.

She gave the clerk her father's details. 'He's gasping for breath and I believe he needs urgent treatment. His medication doesn't seem to be working properly.'

The clerk glanced over to where Katie's father was sitting. 'I'll see if we can have him looked at fairly quickly, Dr Logan. If you'd like to take a seat, I'll have a word with the triage nurse.'

'Thanks.' Katie went back to her father and sat down. 'We shouldn't have to wait too long,' she told him. 'Just try to relax.'

In fact, it was only a matter of minutes before they were called to go into the doctor's room, and Katie was startled to see Nick coming along the corridor to greet them. He looked immaculate, as ever, with dark trousers that moulded his long legs, a crisp linen shirt in a deep shade of blue, and a tie that gave him a businesslike, professional appearance.

She hadn't expected to run into him so soon after their meeting at the hotel. It threw her, coming across him this way, and for a moment or two she wasn't sure how to respond.

'I didn't realise that you worked here,' she said, frowning. 'I'd somehow imagined that you worked at one of the bigger city hospitals.'

He smiled. 'I prefer this one. It has all the up-to-date-facilities, and I've been familiar with it since childhood. It's become like a second home to me.'

He lent her father a supporting shoulder. 'I'm sorry to see that you're having problems, Jack,' he murmured. 'We'll go along to my office where we can be more private.' He turned and called for a nurse. 'Can we get some oxygen here, please?'

'Of course.' The nurse hurried away to find a trolley, while Nick led the way to his office.

Nick waved Katie to a leather-backed chair by the desk, and then turned his attention to Jack.

'Let me help you onto the examination couch,' he said quietly, pumping the bed to an accessible height and assisting Jack into a sitting position, propped up by pillows. 'I see you have your inhaler with you. Is it helping?'

Jack shook his head. 'Not much.' He leaned back against the pillows and tried to gather his breath. His features were drawn, his lips taking on a bluish tinge.

Nick handed him the oxygen mask and carefully fitted it over his nose and mouth. 'Take a few deep breaths,' he said. 'We'll soon have you feeling better, don't worry.'

Katie watched as Nick examined her father. He was very thorough, listening to his chest, taking his blood pressure and pulse and asking questions about the medication he was taking. All the time he was efficient, yet gentle, and she could see that he was a doctor who would put a patient's mind at ease whatever the circumstances. He set up a monitor so that he could check Jack's heart rate and blood oxygen levels. Katie saw that the results were way out of line with what they should be.

'Excuse me for a moment,' Nick murmured. 'I'm going to ask the nurse to bring a nebuliser in here. We'll add a bronchodilator and a steroid to the mix to reduce the inflammation in your airways, and that should soon make you feel a lot more comfortable.'

He went to the door and spoke to the nurse then returned a minute or two later, coming to stand beside the couch once more. 'Your blood pressure is raised,' he said, 'so I think we need to adjust your tablets to bring that down...and also perhaps we should question what's happening to bring that about.'

'I dare say I can give you an answer on that one,' Katie remarked under her breath. Her tone was cynical, and that must have alerted Nick, because he began to walk towards her, obviously conscious that she wouldn't want her father to hear.

'You know what's causing it?' he asked.

'I think so. You and your father have been pushing him to sell the vineyard, and he's worried about making the right decision. It's tearing him apart, thinking about giving up the one thing that has kept him going all these years.'

Nick raised dark brows. 'You're blaming my father and me?' He, too, spoke in a lowered voice.

'I am. Who else would I blame?' She returned his gaze steadily. 'His health is failing, yet you bombarded him with paperwork and tried to persuade him to hand it over. He was looking at the papers this morning when he was taken ill. The vineyard means everything to him, and you've set him a huge dilemma. I don't believe he's in any state to be dealing with matters such as this.'

'I hardly think you can lay the blame at our feet. Jack has been ill for a number of years, and his lung function is way below par. As to causing him any distress, all I can say is that if he didn't want to consider our offer, he only had to say so.' His eyes darkened. 'He's perfectly capable of making his own decisions.'

Katie stiffened. He hadn't added 'without his daughter's interference', but the implication was there, all the same.

The nurse appeared just then with a trolley, and Nick broke off to go and set up the nebuliser. 'Just try to relax and breathe deeply,' he told her father, his manner soothing. 'It'll take a few minutes, but your blood oxygen levels should gradually start to rise. In the meantime, I'm going to go and glance through your medical notes and see where we can make changes to your medication.' He halted as a thought had occurred to him. 'Katie's obviously concerned about you. Do you mind if I discuss your medical history with her, or is it something you would rather I kept private?'

Jack shook his head. 'That's fine. Go ahead. There's nothing to hide.'

'Okay.' Nick checked the monitor once more, before saying quietly, 'I'll also arrange an urgent appointment for you with your respiratory specialist.'

'Thanks,' Jack said. He looked exhausted and seemed relieved to be able to just lie back and let the drugs do their work.

Nick came back to the desk and glanced towards Katie as he sat down.

'He should start to feel better once his airways expand.' He accessed her father's medical notes on the computer, and then said quietly, 'You seem very concerned over this matter of the vineyard. Have you been out to see it?'

She nodded. 'He took me on a tour a few days ago. I was very impressed, completely bowled over by it, in fact. So much work has gone into making it what it is now. It's something to be proud of.' She looked at him through narrowed eyes. 'I can't see any reason why he would want to let it go.'

His mouth made a crooked shape. 'I'd say it was possibly becoming too much for him to handle, but it's probably better if we leave off that discussion for a while. It isn't getting either of us anywhere, is it?'

She clamped her lips shut. Nick glanced at her briefly, and then said, 'Your father's heart is taking a lot of strain—the effect of years of lung disease.' He lowered his voice as he studied her. 'I wonder if you realise just how precarious his situation is becoming.'

She nodded, her mouth making a downward turn. 'I'd guessed. I suppose I just needed to have it confirmed.'

He checked the drug schedule for a moment or two on the computer, and then stood up and went back to her father. 'How are you feeling?' he asked.

'Much better.' Jack managed a smile. 'You've taken good care of me, as always. Thank you for that.'

'You're welcome. It's what I'm here for.' Nick glanced down at his chart. 'I want to prescribe some tablets to ease the workload on your heart, and I think we'll arrange for you to have oxygen at home. If you give me a few minutes, I'll go and see if the respiratory specialist is around. It's possible he might be able to come and see you while you're here, and that way we can finalise the details of your medication in one go.'

'Okay.' Jack nodded. 'I'm not going anywhere for a while.'

Katie could see that he was looking much better. 'The colour is coming back into your face,' she said, going over to him as Nick left the room. 'You had me worried there for a while.'

His glance trailed over her. 'You worry too much. Your mother was the same. I used to say to her, life's too short to be fretting about this and that. Seize the day—as they say. Make the most of it where you can.'

Katie's mouth flattened. 'I suppose that was back in the days when you were getting along with one another...before it all went wrong.'

'I... Yes...' He hesitated, shooting her a quick, cautious glance. 'It hasn't been easy for you, has it, Katie? We tried to make a go of things, you know, your mother and I, but there were problems... For one thing, my job took me away from home so much.'

Katie was unconvinced. 'Your job obviously meant more to you than we did, because one day you went away and never came back.' Even now, her heart lurched at the memory. 'Mum was devastated, and I could never understand why you left us that way. You were living thousands of miles from us. I was eight years old, and suddenly I'd lost my father, and my mother was in pieces. You disappeared from our lives. For a long time I thought I'd done something wrong and it was all my fault that you'd gone away.'

He frowned, his grey eyes troubled. 'I'm sorry, Katie.

I should have handled things differently; I know that now.' He pulled in a deep breath. 'But your mother and I were going through a bad time, and the atmosphere was incredibly tense between us. There were lots of bitter arguments. Back then I thought it would be for the best if I stayed away. I thought it would be easier, less painful.'

She gave a short, harsh laugh. 'You were wrong. It might have been better for you, maybe, but as far as I was concerned a card here and there at birthdays and Christmas was hardly going to make up for the lack of a father. Did you really think it would? And as for presents that you sent—well, they were great but it just made me realise that you didn't even know me. I appreciated the gifts, but I couldn't help thinking that a visit would have been more to the point. But it never happened. I thought perhaps you didn't care.'

It was as though her words had cut into him like a knife. He caught his breath and seemed to slump a little, his features becoming ashen, and Katie looked on in dismay, a rush of guilt running through her. What was she thinking of, having this discussion with him in here, of all places? She had gone too far...way too far. He might have a lot to answer for, but he was ill, after all, and she was layering him with anxiety that could bring on respiratory collapse. She ought to have known better.

'That was thoughtless of me,' she said in an anxious voice. 'I didn't mean to do anything to aggravate your condition.'

'It's all right.' He paused, sucking in another breath. 'It was something I struggled with all the time—leaving you. I kept meaning to come back to see you, but somehow the longer I left it, the harder it became. I thought...if I came back to see you...' he started to gasp, fighting against the constriction in his lungs '...you might be all the more upset if I left you once more. You were very young.'

Katie's expression was bleak. 'Let's not talk about it for the moment. You're ill, and we should concentrate on making you more comfortable. Keep the mask over your face. Take deep breaths and try to relax.'

'What's going on here?' Nick came into the room and hurried over to the bed. 'What happened?' He checked the monitor, and Katie could see that her father's heart rate and respiratory rate had increased to dangerous levels.

'It was... We were just talking. It's my fault,' she said in a halting tone. 'I said some things I shouldn't have said.' She had berated Nick for causing her father stress, and then she had done exactly the same thing, hadn't she?

She pressed her lips together. Wasn't this all part of the problem she had battled with since she had come out here? There was so much resentment locked up inside her, but none of it could gain release...not when her father was so ill. It was frustrating, an ongoing dilemma that could have no end. No matter what he had done, she would have to be inhuman to ignore his condition, wouldn't she?

'No, no...you mustn't blame yourself,' her father said, cutting in on her thoughts. 'It's only right that you should say what's on your mind. I let you down.'

Nick gave her a thoughtful glance. Perhaps he was curious about what was going on between them, but he said nothing. Instead he checked the monitors once more and handed her father a couple of tablets and a drinking cup. 'Take these,' he said. 'They'll bring your blood pressure down and calm your heart rate. Then you need to rest.' He sent Katie a warning glance and her face flushed with heat.

'It isn't Katie's fault,' Jack said, after he had swallowed the tablets. 'The old ticker isn't what it used to be. There isn't much more that you doctors can do for me—you know it, and I know it.'

'I never give up on a patient,' Nick said, his tone firm. 'You'll be fine if you take things easy. Lie back and give the medicine time to take effect.'

They sat with her father for several more minutes, watching as his breathing slowly became easier.

'I feel much better now,' he said, after a while. 'I'll be okay.'

'Maybe, but you can stay where you are for a bit longer,' Nick told him. 'The specialist will be stopping by as soon as he's finished dealing with a patient. He'll sort out your medication and make sure that you're in a good enough condition to go home.'

His pager went off and he turned to Katie. 'I have to go and deal with an emergency that's coming in,' he said. 'Maybe we could meet up some time soon for coffee or dinner? I feel there are things we need to talk about.'

He was probably thinking of her father's illness, and she acknowledged that with a slight inclination of her head. 'Actually, I have the test results on Mrs Wyatt, back in my office—the lady who fell and injured herself at your hotel. She gave me permission to share them with you, although I haven't had time to look at them properly yet. I suppose we should arrange a time to get together to talk about them.'

He nodded. 'Would it be too much of an imposition for you to come over to my beach house with them, say, later this afternoon? I have to be there because I have some people coming to do some work in the courtyard. Just say if it's a problem for you.'

She thought about it and then shook her head. 'It's not a problem. I'm off duty, and you don't live too far from my place.'

'That's great. I'll see you then.' He glanced towards her father. 'I'm glad you're feeling better, Jack. Take care. I'll see you again before too long, I expect.'

He left the room, and Jack sent Katie a questioning look. 'There was a problem at the hotel?'

She nodded and explained what had happened. 'I think he's worried in case the woman or her relatives decide to take it to court. They might try to say her fall was the fault of the hotel proprietor.'

He frowned. 'I can see how he would be worried. It won't simply be the effect this might have on trade at the hotel—the Bellinis have always taken pride in doing the right thing. Nick's father is ultra-traditional in that respect. Everything has to be done the proper way. He's a very private man, and he deplores any negative publicity.'

'I can imagine. But so far they've managed to keep things quiet, and anyway there's a lot riding on the results of various tests that were carried out at the lab.'

'And now he wants you to take the results over to the house?' Jack sent her a thoughtful glance. 'Do I detect more than just a professional collaboration going on here?'

Katie's eyes widened at the question, and she gave a faint shrug of her shoulders. 'You heard what he said. It's just easier this way.'

She wasn't going to say any more on that score. Her father hadn't earned the right to intervene in her private life, had he? Besides, how could she possibly answer him when she didn't know for sure herself what had prompted the invitation? The deed had been accomplished before she'd had time to give it much thought.

Jack was frowning. 'I could see that he was interested in you from the outset…but you should be careful how you go, with him, Katie. I know you're still recovering from what went on back in the UK, and I wouldn't want to see you hurt all over again.'

He halted for a second or two to allow his lungs to recover. 'Nick Bellini's a law unto himself where women are concerned. They seem to fall for him readily enough, but he's never yet settled down with any of them. Don't go getting your heart broken over the likes of him. He's a fine doctor—he's kept an eye on me over the last few years, just because he was concerned for me—and he's a great businessman, a wonderful friend and associate, but he's lethal to the fairer sex.'

Katie frowned. He was only telling her what she'd already guessed. That newspaper headline that had been bugging her for the last few days suddenly swam into her head once more, and this time she could see it with perfect clarity. *'Tearful heiress Shannon Draycott leaves hotel under cover of darkness. Bellini tycoon declines to comment.'* There had been more. The article had said something about a broken engagement, and there had been a lot of conjecture, along with several interviews with friends of the young woman. They all painted a picture of a tragic heiress who had been left in the lurch.

'Well, thanks for warning me. I'll be sure to keep it in mind.'

Was Nick a man who was afraid of commitment, flitting from one woman to another? Katie was determined not to get involved with anyone like that ever again. She had been devastated when her relationship with James had ended. She had trusted him and believed they might have had a future together, but it had all gone terribly wrong, and now she would do everything she could to steer clear of any man who might cause her pain.

She studied her father. He was an enigma. He looked gaunt, with prominent cheekbones and dark shadows under his eyes, and something in her made her want to reach out to him and wrap her arms around him. It was confusing.

All those years he had stayed away, removing himself from her life, and yet now he was acting like a protective father, as though her well-being was suddenly important to him. She couldn't quite work him out. For so long she had tried not to think about him at all. He had walked out on her and her mother and she couldn't forgive him for that…and yet now her emotions were torn.

Little by little, as she came to know him better, he was beginning to tug at her heartstrings. She didn't know how it had happened, but she felt sorry for him and in spite of herself she was worried about him. He looked so thin and wasted, and it occurred to her that he probably wasn't eating as well as he should.

As for Nick Bellini, she'd already learned to be wary of him, and she had to be grateful that her father had let her know what she was up against. Anyway, surely her fears were groundless? Her relationship with Nick was going to be strictly professional, wasn't it?

It didn't surprise her one bit to discover that he had the reputation of a compulsive heartbreaker.

A couple of hours later, Katie dropped her father off at his house and left him in the care of Libby, his house-keeper. 'I'll keep an eye on him, don't you worry,' the woman said, and Katie immediately felt reassured. Libby was kindly and capable looking, and Katie knew she was leaving him in good hands.

Then she set off for Nick's beach house. The scenery was breathtaking as she drove along, with the sun glint-ing on the blue Pacific Ocean and the rugged length of the coastline stretching out ahead of her.

Living here was like being dropped into a secluded corner of paradise, she reflected as she parked her car in Nick's driveway a few minutes later. She slid out of the car and looked around, gazing out over the bay and watching the surf form lacy white ribbons on the sand. Black oystercatchers moved busily amongst the rocks, seeking out mussels and molluscs with their long orange beaks.

'Katie, I'm glad you could make it,' Nick said, coming out of the house to greet her. 'I was on the upper deck when I saw you arrive.' His arms closed around her in a welcoming hug, and in spite of herself her senses im-mediately responded in a flurry of excitement. 'How's your father?' he asked.

'Much better.'

'I'm glad.'

His arms were warm and strong, folding her to him, and for a wild moment or two she was tempted to nestle against him and accept the shelter he offered. She could feel the reassuring, steady beat of his heart through the thin cotton of her top.

'It's good to see you,' he murmured, stepping back a little to look at her. 'I hope you didn't mind coming out here to visit me—it's just that I have to be at the house to oversee some work I'm having done out back, as I told you. The workmen are installing a hot tub in the courtyard.'

'That sounds like fun,' she said, easing herself away from him. She ran a hand over her jeans in a defensive gesture, smoothing the denim. This closeness was doing strange things to her heart rate, and it wouldn't do to have him see what effect he was having on her. 'You certainly have the climate for it out here.'

He smiled, his hand slipping to her waist as he gently led her towards the house. 'I'm looking forward to trying it out. All those jets of water are supposed to make you feel really good, like a soothing massage.' He grinned. 'Perhaps you might like to try it with me some time?'

'I…uh…' She gave a soft intake of breath. 'I'd have to think about that.' She blinked. The prospect of sharing a hot tub with him was much more than she could handle right then. In fact, she'd have to know him a whole lot better before anything like that ever happened.

He laughed softly. 'I'll take that as a definite maybe,' he said. 'Let me show you around the house.'

'Thank you. I'd like that.' She gazed at the beautiful building as they walked along the path. It was multi-storeyed, with sloping roofs at varying levels, the tiles a soft sandstone colour that contrasted perfectly with the white-painted walls. There were arched windows and glass doors, and there were steps leading from a balconied terrace on the upper floor, providing external access to the ground below. Behind the whole edifice was a backdrop of green Monterey pines, and in the far distance she could see lush, forested mountain slopes. 'This is fantastic,' she murmured. 'It's a spectacular house.'

She turned to look back at the Pacific. 'I really envy you, living out here by the ocean. It must be lovely to look out over the water every day and gaze at the cliffs that form the bay.'

'It's very relaxing. I know I'm fortunate to be able to enjoy it.' He showed her into the house, and they stepped into a wide entrance hall whose pale-coloured walls reflected the light. The oak floor gleamed faintly.

He led the way into a room just off the hall. 'This is the lounge, as you can see. I tend to sit in here to read the paper or watch TV of an evening. It's a very peaceful room, and it looks out over the patio garden. And, of course, with the French doors it's handy for the courtyard…and, from now on, the hot tub, too,' he added with a grin.

She peered out through the open doors at the court-yard that was closed in on three sides by different wings of the building. The remaining side was made up of a decorative screen wall, providing a glimpse into the garden beyond. 'I can see the men are still working on it. It looks as though you have everything you need out there—a place to relax and enjoy the sunshine, a barbecue area, and all those lovely flowers and shrubs to enjoy. It looks like a little piece of heaven.'

She turned to gaze around the room. 'I like the pale-coloured furnishings in here, too. It just adds to the feel-ing of light.' Her glance took in glass shelves and a low table, before trailing over the sumptuous sofa and chairs. Pastel-coloured cushions added a delicate touch.

'I'm glad you like it,' he said, claiming her hand and leading her through an open doorway. 'Let me show you the kitchen, and I'll make us a drink. What would you like—coffee, tea? You could have iced tea, if you prefer. Or maybe you'd like something stronger?'

'Iced tea sounds fine, thanks.' She stopped to look around. 'Oh, this is lovely,' she said with a soft gasp. 'And it's such a large room, too.' The cupboards and wall units were all finished in the palest green, verging on white, and marble worktops gleamed palely in the sunlight that poured in through the windows. There were shelves filled with bright copper pans, and corner wall units with attractive ceramics on display.

'Well, it serves as a breakfast kitchen,' Nick explained, going over to the fridge. 'There's a separate dining room through the archway, but I tend to eat in here, mostly...or upstairs on the upper deck. I can look out over the ocean from there.'

'That sounds like bliss.'

He nodded, putting ice into two glasses and adding tea from a jug. 'It is. Would you like lemon and mint with this?' he asked, indicating the iced tea.

'Please. That would be good.'

He placed the two glasses on a tray, along with the jug of tea and a plate of mixed hors d'oeuvres. 'We'll take these upstairs and I'll show you the upper deck. 'It's great up there at this time of day, and you can see over the whole of the bay from the terrace.'

She followed him up the stairs, walking through a second sitting room and out through beautifully embellished glass doors onto the balcony terrace.

He was right. The view from the deck was fantastic, and Katie could even see the wildflowers that grew on the craggy slopes in the distance. He pulled out a chair for her by a wrought-iron table, and she sat down and began to relax.

Out here, there were tubs of yellow and orange California poppies, their silky petals moving gently in the faint breeze, and against the far wall, standing tall alongside a trellis, were spiky blue delphiniums. Hanging baskets provided even more colour, with exuberant displays of petunias.

'Help yourself to food,' he said, sliding a plate across the table towards her. 'I wasn't sure whether you would have eaten or not before you came.'

'Thanks.' She glanced at the food on display. There was pâté with crackers, honey-glazed chicken and a spicy tomato dip with tortilla chips. 'It looks delicious.'

He smiled. 'Not my doing, I'm afraid. I have food sent over from the hotel quite often. I don't always have time to cook.'

'I'm not surprised. You must spend the bulk of your time at the hospital, and even if you don't work on a day-to-day basis at the vineyard or the hotel, there must be a fair amount of organisational work to deal with. I expect you're the one who has to make the most important decisions, aren't you?'

He nodded. 'That's true. Things tend to crop up from time to time that need my attention—like this unfortunate episode with Mrs Wyatt.' He frowned. 'I went to see her, and I'm really pleased that she's looking a lot better than she was a few days ago.'

Katie smiled. 'Yes. I couldn't help noticing that you arranged for her to have a private room—the basket of fruit and the flowers you sent were a lovely touch. I know she appreciated them.'

'It was the least I could do.' He spread pâté onto a cracker and bit into it. 'People come to the hotel expecting to have a good time and live for a while in the lap of luxury. They don't want to find themselves being taken out of there by ambulance.'

'But you weren't obliged to pay anything towards her hospital care, were you?'

He shrugged. 'No, that's true. Her insurance company will pay for that…but I wanted to be certain she had the upgrade to make sure that she's comfortable, and, anyway, I count it as good customer relations.'

'Hmm. I can see that you take your role as hotelier seriously.' She dipped a tortilla chip into the fiery salsa sauce. 'You must be anxious to know what caused Mrs Wyatt to fall and break her shoulder. Would you like to hear the results of the tests?'

'Yes, definitely… I'm glad she said it would be all right for you to discuss them with me. Is it what we thought—a TIA?'

She nodded. 'It looks that way. The doctors monitored her heart and discovered that she has atrial fibrillation—as you know, that kind of abnormal heart rhythm can sometimes cause clots to form in the blood vessels. They did a CT scan, along with blood tests, and found a narrowing of the arteries. The general feeling is that she probably developed a blood clot that temporarily disturbed the flow of blood to the brain. This most likely dissolved of its own accord, but it's possible that more will form as time progresses if she doesn't have treatment.'

'So presumably they have her on anti-thrombotic

therapy? And they'll give her medication to counteract the abnormal heart rhythm?'

'That's right.' She took a sip of iced tea. 'It looks as though you're in the clear—or, should I say, the hotel's in the clear?' She smiled at him. 'That must be a huge relief to you.'

'Yes, it is. I can't tell you how badly I needed to hear that. It's great news. Lucky, too, for Mrs Wyatt, because now she gets to have the treatment she needs to put her back on the road to health.' He rested back in his seat, taking a swallow of iced tea and looking the picture of contentment. 'Thanks for telling me that, Katie. I'm really obliged to you for finding out all this information.'

He set down his glass and looked her over, leaning towards her. 'In fact, if I didn't think you'd take it amiss, I could kiss you for it.' He came closer, as though, having hit on the idea, he was ready to carry it through into immediate action, regardless of the consequences.

Katie flattened herself against the back of her chair, deftly foiling his attempt. 'I think you'd better give that one a miss,' she said, her green gaze meshing with his. 'It wouldn't do if every male doctor tried to kiss me whenever I presented them with good results, would it?'

His eyes narrowed. 'Have any tried?'

'Oh, yes. From time to time.'

'And succeeded?' He was frowning now, his blue eyes darkening.

'Maybe. Once or twice.' His expression crystallised into one of seething frustration, and she laughed softly. 'Sorry about that. I couldn't resist. You looked so put out.'

He gazed at her, totally nonplussed. 'You certainly got me going there,' he said, his mouth twisting. 'My fault. I should have known any number of men would want to try their luck with you. That goes for me, too. Somehow, ever since we first met, I've been hung up on getting to know you better...much better.'

She pulled a face. 'Well, I'm not sure that's such a good idea—not in the way you mean, at least.'

He studied her thoughtfully for a moment or two, his expression serious. 'He hurt you badly, didn't he—this man from back home? You must have been very much in love with him.'

'I thought I was,' she said awkwardly. 'I thought I knew him, but perhaps I was blind to his faults. He had a lot of charisma, and I believed he was saving it all for me. It turned out I was wrong.'

And wasn't Nick so very much like James? He had that scintillating charm that could sweep a woman off her feet, and Katie was no exception. She had to be on her guard. No matter how hard he tried, she wasn't going to succumb to Nick's winning ways. Hadn't her father warned her about him?

'But let's not dwell on any of that,' she murmured. 'I'm here with you now, and we do have two things in common...our work and my father. Maybe it would be safer all round if we simply kept things between us on that level.'

'Hmm...maybe.' He sounded doubtful. His eyes were still dark, and there was a brooding quality to his expression.

Katie decided to plough on with her new diversionary tactic. She helped herself to some food and said quietly, 'Perhaps we should talk about what happened this morning—about your efforts to persuade my father to sell his land, and the effect it's having on him. Maybe we need to clear the air on that score. You know I'd sooner you put an end to any attempt at making a deal. Anyway, I have the feeling he's not at all sure about going ahead with it.'

Nick frowned. 'He hasn't said as much to me...and while there's a chance he'll concede to us, we're bound to keep trying. It would mean a lot to my father to bring the vineyard back into our keeping. My great-great-grandfather bought the land at the turn of the century, but a parcel of it was sold off some years back when the family fell on hard times. It's a matter of pride to my father to restore the vineyards into family owner-ship once more. He sees it as our inheritance. It's very important to him.'

'That may be so, but I can't say it any clearer—I think you should hold off on those negotiations.'

Nick's steady gaze met hers. 'Jack doesn't need you to hold his hand where business is concerned.'

A glint of steel came into Katie's eyes. 'I have to dis-agree with you on that one,' she said. 'And this is defi-nitely not the right time to be pursuing it with him.'

Nick frowned. 'That's another matter, of course. We both saw how ill he was today.' He poured more iced tea into her glass. 'You think your father needs to be cosseted but he takes it on himself to take care of busi-ness matters, and then it becomes a matter of pride for him to see things through.'

So, no matter what she said, he wasn't giving up on his plan to secure her father's land. She drank her iced tea and studied him over the rim of her glass. Clearly, his family was not going to be satisfied with the empire they had built up. They would go after whatever they wanted. Forewarned was forearmed.

Nick's phone bleeped, and he glanced down at the screen briefly. 'It looks as though the workmen have finished installing the hot tub,' he said. 'Shall we go down and take a look?'

'Yes, of course.'

She followed him down the stairs and out to the courtyard, where the workmen waited, standing by their handiwork.

'We're all done here,' the spokesman said. 'I think you'll find everything's in order. Just turn these controls here to adjust the jets.' He began to point out the various buttons and fittings. 'This is your filter...and here's where you change the heat settings. We've left it set to around midway. Neither too hot nor too cold, but of course it's all a matter of personal preference.'

'That's great,' Nick murmured. 'It looks perfect. Thanks for all your hard work.' He turned to Katie. 'Stay and enjoy the courtyard for a minute or two, will you, while I go and see the men off? There's an ornamental fishpond that you might like to look at, over there in the corner. I'll be back in a few minutes.'

'Okay.' She watched him go, then turned and walked towards the far side of the courtyard, an attractive area, laid out with a trellised arbour and rockery. A gentle waterfall splashed into the pond where koi carp swam amongst the plants and hid beneath white waterlilies.

She gazed down at the green fronds of water plants drifting with the ripple of water from a small fountain and lost herself for a while in a reverie of a past life.

'Sorry to have left you,' Nick said, coming back to her a short time later. 'I think the men did a good job.

They sited the tub perfectly and left the place looking neat and tidy. Didn't take them too long either.'

She nodded. 'I expect you'll appreciate your new tub for a good many years to come.' Turning back to the pond, she added, 'This is beautifully set out. The water's so clear, and the plants are perfect.' Her voice became wistful. 'I remember having one in our garden when I was a child...but it was never as good as this. I suppose you have to keep on top of things—make sure the filter is kept clear, and so on.'

'That's true. I tend to check it every so often. The pond is a hobby of mine. I find it totally relaxing, something you need so that you can wind down after a day in Emergency.' He sent her an oblique glance. 'Did your father set up your pond...or was it something that came with the house, so to speak?'

'It came with the house. My father was interested in it, but he wasn't around for long enough to take care of it, and the work fell to my mother.'

'And she wasn't that keen?'

'She was keen enough when my father was with us, but after he left to go and live here in California she fell apart. She lost interest in everything.'

He frowned. 'I'm sorry. That must have been hard.' He scanned her face thoughtfully. 'I've known Jack for some eighteen years, ever since he pipped us to the post and bought the vineyard from its previous owner. In all that time I had no idea he had a daughter back in the UK.'

'No. It seems he kept it quiet.'

'I suppose you had to take a lot of the burden on your shoulders—how old were you when he left?'

'I was eight. As to any burden, I must say I didn't

really understand what was going on at the time. It was all very confusing. When I realised he wasn't coming back, I was hurt, heartbroken, and then as the years went by I became angry and resentful. There was just my mother and me, no cosy family unit with brothers and sisters to share happy times. I missed that.'

A shadow crossed his eyes. 'And that's why you never came over here until now.' He looked at her with new understanding. 'You were waiting for him to come back to you.'

She lowered her head. 'It wasn't going to happen, was it? So eventually I decided that if I was to make peace with myself, I had to come and find him and sort out my demons once and for all.'

He slid an arm around her shoulders. 'I'm sorry that you had to go through all that,' he said quietly. 'It must have been a terrible time for you.' He drew her close and pressed a light kiss on her forehead. 'It seems almost unforgivable that he should treat you that way, and yet I know Jack is a good man at heart.'

Katie didn't answer. She couldn't. She was too conscious of his nearness, and it brought up all kinds of conflicting emotions within her. Everything in her told her that this man was some kind of adversary. He was a threat to her father, and a danger to her peace of mind, and yet when he touched her like this, she was instantly lost in a cotton-wool world of warmth and comfort.

His arms were around her, his body shielding hers from all that might hurt her, and the searing impact of that tender kiss had ricocheted throughout her whole body. She didn't want to move, or speak. Why couldn't she stay here, locked in his embrace, where the world stood still and she might forget her worries?

'Do you think you can find it in you to forgive him?' Nick murmured. 'He's very ill, and there may not be too much time left.'

'I don't know.' She gave a faint sigh. The spell was broken and she straightened, gazing down into the water of the pond. Fish darted among the green fronds, oblivious to the troubles of the world around them. If only she could find such inner peace.

She took a step backwards. 'I should go,' she said. Nick was the last person she should look to for comfort. He could well turn out to be even more of a heartbreaker than her father.

CHAPTER FOUR

'Is YOUR father really considering selling his vineyard to the Bellini family? That seems very strange to me.' Eve Logan sounded doubtful at the other end of the line. 'I haven't had a lot of contact with him over these last few years, but I did gain the impression that the business meant an awful lot to him. I wouldn't have thought it was something he would give it up lightly.'

'No, probably not,' Katie agreed. 'When I spoke to him the other day he said he hadn't thought it through yet, or words to that effect. I'm wondering if the Bellinis are putting undue pressure on him. He isn't well, and I have the strong feeling that he isn't up to it.'

'Then perhaps it's as well that you're over there and able to look out for him.'

'Yes, maybe.'

Katie cut the call to her mother a few minutes later and gazed around the apartment. She was feeling oddly restless. Ever since her visit to Nick's home several days ago, she had been suffering from what she could only think of as withdrawal symptoms, and it was all Nick's fault.

That kiss had been the lightest, gentlest touch, and it surely had been nothing more than a gesture of comfort and understanding, but the memory of it had stayed with her ever since. Nick had a compelling, magnetic charm that could surely melt the stoniest heart, and she was proving to be no exception.

It wouldn't do at all. She was off men...they could string you along and lead you into thinking that everything was perfect, and then throw it all in your face with the biggest deception of all. No. Every instinct warned her that it would be far better to steer clear of Nick before he could work his magic on her. He spelled trouble and that was something she could definitely do without.

It didn't help that she managed to catch a glimpse of his house every time she headed along the main highway on her way to or from the hospital. Today had been no exception. Nick's home was beautiful, a jewel set in the golden, sand-fringed crown of the California coast.

Annoyingly, against all her better judgement, her thoughts kept straying to him. What was he doing... was he there, sitting outside on the upper deck, watching the seagulls perch on the distant bluffs?

But she wasn't going to waste any more time thinking about him. Enough was enough, and she had work to do. The dishwasher needed emptying and there was a stack of ironing waiting for her...though with any luck she could finish her chores and still have time to wander down to the beach and take in one of the glorious sunsets that were the norm around there.

She set to work, but she was only halfway through her ironing pile when the phone rang.

'There's been a surfing accident just a mile from where you are,' her boss told her. 'Darren Mayfield, a fourteen-year-old, was knocked unconscious and had to be pulled out of the water. The ambulance has been called, but you'll probably reach him before it arrives. A nasty head injury, by all accounts.'

'I'll leave right away,' she told him, unplugging the iron and heading for the door. Her medical bag was in the hall, ready for such emergencies, and the rest of her supplies were in the car.

The boy's level of consciousness was waxing and waning by the time she arrived on the beach. 'Do you know anything about what happened to him?' she asked his mother, who was waiting anxiously by his side.

'He came off his board when one of the big waves hit,' the woman said, her voice shaky. 'The board sort of rose up in the air and then crashed down on him. We had to drag him out of the water. There's a gash on the back of his head and he's bleeding… He hasn't come round properly since we brought him to shore.' Her lips trembled. 'He keeps being sick, and I thought it was just concussion, but it's more than that, isn't it? He should have recovered by now.'

'I'll take a look,' Katie murmured, kneeling down beside the boy. 'How are you doing, Darren?' she asked quietly. 'Can you hear me?' She waited, and when there was no response she added, 'Do you know what happened to you?'

He still didn't answer, and Katie began to make a swift but thorough examination. 'He's unconscious,' she told his mother, after a while. 'I'm going to put a tube down his throat, and give him oxygen, to help with his breathing, and then I need to stabilise his spine to prevent any more damage being done.' She carefully put a cervical collar in place, before checking the boy's heart rate once more. It was worryingly low, and his blood pressure was high, both signs that the pressure within his brain was rising. That didn't bode well.

Suddenly, Darren's whole body began to shake, and Katie reached in her medical bag for a syringe.

'Why's he doing that?' his mother asked in a panicked voice. 'What's happening to him?'

'He's having a seizure,' Katie answered. It was yet another indication that this boy was in trouble. 'I'm going to inject him with medication that will help to stop the fit.'

By the time the paramedics arrived, she had put in place an intravenous line so that fluids and any further drugs could be administered swiftly and easily. 'We need spinal support here,' she told the men, keeping her voice low so as not to worry the boy's mother any further. 'He has a depressed skull fracture, so we need to phone ahead and tell the trauma team what to expect. They'll most likely need to prepare him for Theatre.'

She spoke to the lead paramedic as they wheeled Darren into the ambulance a few minutes later. 'I'll ride along with him in case there are any more complications along the way.'

The paramedic nodded. 'You go ahead with Mrs Mayfield and sit by him. I'll call the emergency department and keep them up to date.'

'Thanks.'

Katie looked at her patient. He was deathly pale and she was deeply concerned for this boy as she sat beside him in the ambulance. She had placed a temporary dressing on the wound at the back of his head, but it was bleeding still, and she was worried about the extent of the damage.

The journey to the hospital seemed to take for ever,

though in reality it was probably only about fifteen minutes, and as soon as they pulled into the ambulance bay, Katie was ready to move. The paramedics wheeled Darren towards the main doors.

'He had another seizure in the ambulance,' she told the doctor who came out to greet them, 'so I've boosted the anti-convulsive therapy. I'm afraid his blood pressure is high and it looks as though the intracranial pressure is rising.' Again, she spoke quietly so that the boy's mother wouldn't be unduly alarmed, but to her relief a nurse stepped forward and gently took the woman to one side.

'We'll get an x-ray just as soon as we've managed to stabilise his blood pressure,' a familiar voice said, and Katie was startled to see Nick appear at the side of the trolley. He was wearing green scrubs that only seemed to emphasise the muscular strength of his long, lean body. Her heart gave a strange little lurch.

He listened attentively to the paramedic's report and was already checking the patient's vital signs, scanning the readings on the portable heart monitor that Katie had set up. Then he looked at Katie and gave her a quick smile. 'Hi,' he said.

'Oh… I…somehow I hadn't expected to see you here.' Katie's response was muted, but she recovered herself enough to acknowledge him, and also the paramedics, who were ready to leave on another callout. She was troubled about her patient's progress, but Nick's sudden appearance had thrown her way off balance. In the heat of the moment it had completely slipped her mind that he might be on duty.

'I'm on the late shift today,' he told her, as if in answer to her unspoken thoughts, as they moved towards the trauma room. His glance ran quickly over her. 'It's great to see you again.'

'Likewise,' she said, and then tacked on hurriedly, 'I'd like to stay with Darren to see how he goes, if that's all right with you?'

'That'll be fine.' By now they had arrived in the resuscitation room and from then on he concentrated his attention on his patient, examining the boy quickly and telling the nurse who was assisting, 'We'll monitor blood glucose, renal function, electrolytes. I'll take blood for testing now and we need to consult urgently with the neurosurgeon. Given the boy's condition, it's quite likely he'll want to put him on mannitol to reduce the intracranial pressure. Ask him to come down to look at him, will you?'

Katie watched him work. He was remarkably efficient, cool, calm, and obviously concerned for this teenager. He didn't hesitate for an instant, but carried out the necessary procedures with effortless skill, delegating other tasks to members of the team. Then, when the neurosurgeon came to the side of the bed, he spent several minutes talking to him about the boy's condition.

'I'll be ready for him in Theatre in about half an hour,' the surgeon remarked as he prepared to leave the room. 'Let me have the CT images as soon as they're available.'

'Of course.' Nick checked Darren's vital signs once more, and only when he was satisfied that he had done everything possible for the boy did he turn back to Katie.

'Okay, we'll take him along to the CT unit. Let's find out exactly what's going on here.'

As soon as Darren had been placed on the CT trolley,

they went into the annexe to watch the images on the computer screen as the technician began the X-ray. 'You're right,' Nick said, after a few minutes. 'It's a depressed fracture, with the bone fragments pushing down on the lining of the brain. There's a large blood clot causing a build-up of pressure. If we don't act soon, there's a risk that the brain will herniate.'

He spoke to the technician. 'Download the films to the computer in Theatre, will you? Dr Kelso will want to see them.'

The technician nodded, but Nick was already striding out of the annexe towards his patient. 'We'll have to get him to Theatre just as soon as we've cleaned the wound,' he told Katie. 'By that time Mr Kelso should be ready for him.'

They went back to the trauma room and Nick began the process of irrigating the wound while Katie looked on.

'Okay, that should be clean enough now,' he said after a while. 'We'll start him on antibiotics to prevent any infection,' he told the nurse, 'and keep on with the anticonvulsant therapy. In the meantime, give Mr Kelso a call and find out if he's ready for him up in Theatre, will you?'

The nurse nodded. 'Right away.'

A few minutes later when they had the go-ahead, Nick took his patient to the lift. 'Will you be here when I come back?' he asked Katie. 'I'm going to stay with Darren until the operation's over, but it would be good to talk to you some more.'

She nodded. 'I want to see how he does in surgery. Perhaps I should go and talk to Mrs Mayfield? I know Mr Kelso has spoken to her already, but she might appreciate having someone with her to answer any questions.'

'That would be brilliant, if you don't mind. I'm sure you and she have already managed to build up rapport and it'll be good for her to have someone familiar to be with her.'

The lift doors closed behind him, and Katie walked away, heading for the waiting room where Mrs Mayfield was sitting anxiously, hoping for news of her son.

'Can I get you anything?' Katie asked, going to sit beside her. 'A cup of coffee, perhaps?'

Mrs Mayfield shook her head. 'A nurse brought me one already, thank you.' She looked near to tears. 'I've been trying to contact my husband. He was at a conference, but he's coming straight back here now.' She looked at Katie. 'Darren's in a bad way, isn't he? He was unconscious for so long. What's going to happen to him?'

'Darren was unconscious because the impact of the surfboard pushed the bones of his skull inward, causing them to break and press down on the lining of his brain. This damaged some of the blood vessels, so that a blood clot built up quickly between the skull and the lining.'

Mrs Mayfield nodded to show that she understood. 'And this operation that he's having—Mr Kelso said they needed to bring down the pressure. How will they do that?'

'The surgeon will lift up the bone fragments that are pressing down, and at the same time he'll suck out the blood clot.'

'But will he be able to stop the bleeding? Won't the clot build up again?'

'He'll use special materials to repair the blood vessels

so that shouldn't happen. You can be sure that he'll do the very best he can for your son, Mrs Mayfield.' Katie used a reassuring tone, her heart going out to this woman who was petrified for her boy's safety. She couldn't bear to think how she would feel if she had children of her own. It must be the worst thing in the world to know that they were in danger.

She stayed with her for some twenty minutes, until the door opened and Mr Mayfield walked into the room. He went over to his wife and held her tight, both of them fearful and anxious about their son.

Katie left them alone. A nurse would come by and see how they were doing in a while, and now Katie went along to the emergency room to find out if there was any news.

She knew quite a few of the doctors and nurses who worked there by now, from her work as a paediatrician and first responder. Sometimes she had to liaise with them over the phone, and occasionally, as today, she would ride along with the patient and make the handover in person.

'No news yet,' the nurse said, 'but Nick's on his way down from Theatre. He wants us to make preparations to send the boy over to the intensive care unit.'

Katie nodded. 'Thanks for letting me know, Abby. I'll wait by the nurses' station, if that's all right. I really want to know how he does.'

'Of course it is.' She smiled. 'The one consolation is that having you there from the outset must have given the boy at least a sporting chance. Too often, time drags on before people with head injuries have expert treatment. Nick reckons you did a great job.'

Katie gave a bleak smile. 'Let's hope we've all done

enough to make a difference. It's such a devastating experience all round. One minute the boy's out there, enjoying the sunshine and the exhilaration of surfing the waves, and the next, in a freak accident, he's out cold and fighting for his life.' She shook her head. 'I've trained for this, but I don't think I'll ever get used to it.'

'Neither will I,' Abby said.

'You get through it by doing the best you can for your patients,' Nick commented, coming to join them. 'That way you get to sleep easier at night.'

Katie turned to face him, while the nurse left them to go and fetch linen from the supply room. 'Maybe you manage to drop off well enough,' she murmured. 'I can't say that it comes that easily to me.'

'That's a shame.' He draped an arm around her. 'Maybe I could help to remedy that?' he ventured on a husky note. 'Perhaps I could find some way to soothe you to sleep.' He lifted a quizzical brow, looking deep into her eyes.

Katie felt her colour rise. 'In your dreams,' she murmured.

He laughed. 'Well, it was worth a try, I thought.'

'Not really…and I have to say, your timing sucks.' She frowned. 'How is Darren? Did he come through the operation all right?'

His expression sobered. 'Mr Kelso managed to finish the procedure without there being any added complications,' he said. 'The boy's intracranial pressure is at a safer level now, but his blood pressure's still alarmingly high. ICU will monitor him closely, of course. All we can do now is wait and see if he can pull through. He's young and previously in good health, so that's in his favour.' He sent her an encouraging smile. 'The young are quite resilient, as you know. It never ceases to amaze me how they bounce back from even the most traumatic of situations.'

'I'll keep my hopes up for him.' She gazed around the emergency department. 'Everything seems very well co-ordinated around here,' she said. 'The staff all seem to work very well together—I expect that has something to do with the way you run things. You're in charge here, aren't you? Everyone speaks very highly of you.'

'I'm glad of that.' He looked at her from under dark lashes. 'A lot of people, the press especially, seem to think that because I come from a wealthy family I don't need to work and I'm not career orientated, but they couldn't be more wrong. I love my job.'

'I think I've seen that for myself. Though you're right…you do tend to get negative publicity from time to time, don't you?'

He sighed, leaning back against the nurses' station, crossing one long leg over the other at the ankles. 'It seems to be an occupational hazard. If you belong to a family with international holdings, I suppose you're bound to find yourself in the news from time to time.'

She nodded. 'There was a short piece about Mrs Wyatt's accident in the local press, but it was quite favourable. The journalist pointed out that you'd acted swiftly in sending for medical treatment, and that you'd helped make her stay in hospital more comfortable.'

'That's something, at least.' He made a wry smile. 'My father employs a spokesman to deal with the press. It helps to dispel any of the more outlandish stories, and gives the public our take on events.'

'Perhaps your spokesman wasn't around when the

Shannon Draycott story broke?' she said softly. 'That must have caused you a few uneasy moments.'

His mouth turned down at the corners. 'I see you've been discovering my lurid past. No wonder you keep fending me off. I expect you're one of these people who believe everything you read in the papers?'

She shrugged lightly. 'Not necessarily. Though I do go along with the principle that there's no smoke without fire.' He hadn't exactly denied the story, had he? According to the papers, they had been engaged to be married—what kind of man was he that could make light of such a thing?

He winced. 'Then I'm obviously doomed.' A glint of amusement came into his eyes. 'Is there anything I can do to restore your confidence in me? I'm really one of the good guys, you know. And when I spoke to Shannon last week she seemed reasonably content with the way her life was going.'

So he was still in touch with her. The thought sounded a death knell in Katie's mind to any hopes that the stories might be a figment of someone's imagination. 'I'm glad to hear it. Perhaps she counts herself lucky to have escaped.'

'Ouch!' He clamped a hand to his chest and pretended to stagger. 'That was a well-aimed blow. I didn't realise Dr Katie Logan had such a cutting edge...though I suppose you've sharpened up your defences this last year or so.'

She nodded. 'You can count on it.' After her experience with James, she was well prepared, and on her guard, for men who had hidden secrets and a good deal of charm.

'Hmm.' He studied her thoughtfully. 'So what am I

to do to persuade you that things are not as they seem? Do you think spending more time with me would help you to get to know me better?'

It was her turn to laugh. 'I have to give you eleven out of ten for trying, anyway. You're irrepressible, aren't you?'

'Where you're concerned, yes, I am.' His gaze meshed with hers. 'So how about coming along to a wine tasting at the vineyard? We're celebrating a new Pinot Noir this year, one of our finest...and you did say you'd like to see around the vineyard, didn't you? Your father's maybe, but ours is right alongside?'

'I... Um...' She thought things through. Ever since she had seen her father's land, she had been caught up in the wonder of vine culture, and now she was fascinated by everything to do with wine and wine making. She was intrigued to take a look over the Bellini land and see if it was anything like her father's. Where was the harm? It wouldn't be like going on a date, would it? After all, there would be other people around.

'A little wine tasting can be good for the soul,' Nick murmured in a coaxing tone. 'It helps you to look on life with a much more mellow attitude.'

'I'm sure that's true.' She smiled, and against all her best intentions heard herself say, 'Thanks, I think I'd enjoy that.'

. 'That's great news. I'll come and pick you up. Will you be free after work on Wednesday? I have a half-day then.'

'I will,' she murmured. 'I'll look forward to it.'

Later, though, as she waved goodbye to the paramedic who gave her a lift back to her car where she had left it on the coast road, she couldn't help wondering if she was making a mistake. Why, when every part of her knew that she should avoid getting involved with Nick, did she keep digging herself in deeper?

CHAPTER FIVE

'KATIE, Dr Bellini wants to know if you will consult with him on a young patient in the emergency department.' Carla popped her head round the door of Katie's office and waited for an answer. 'I could ask Mike to cover for you here, if you like.'

'Okay. Tell him I'll be along in five minutes.' Katie put the last suture into the cut on a small child's lip. 'There you are, young man, all finished. You've been very brave.' She smiled at the six-year-old and reached into her desk drawer for a colouring sheet and a teddy-bear badge. 'I think you deserve these, don't you?'

The boy gave a tentative nod and studied the piece of paper she'd handed him. 'A racing car!' he exclaimed in delight. 'I'm going to colour it red, and put stripes on the wings.' He looked up at her. 'Thank you.'

'My pleasure.'

She saw the boy and his mother out into the corridor, and then readied herself to go along to the emergency unit, smoothing down her pencil-line skirt and making sure that her blouse neatly skimmed the curve of her hips.

She paused, trying to make sense of her actions. Why was she doing this? Was she really so bothered about meeting up with Nick that she needed to fuss about the way she looked? Unhappily, the answer had to be a resounding 'Yes'. It gave her confidence to know that she looked okay.

A final check in the mirror showed her that her hair was the usual mass of chaotic curls, but there wasn't much she could do about that. At least it was clean and shining.

'Thanks for coming along, Katie.' Nick met her at the door of his office. His glance flicked over her, and an appreciative gleam came into his eyes. 'I'd like you to take a look at young Matthew Goren, if you will. I've asked his mother if she wouldn't mind you giving a second opinion.'

'That's okay. I'm happy to do it.'

He introduced her to the boy's mother and then to Matthew, a thin-looking eleven-year-old who looked uncomfortable and deeply troubled.

'Matt's complaining of pain in his thigh,' Nick said, as they went over to the trolley bed. 'It came on three days ago, and now he's unable to walk because of it. He has a low-grade fever, mild hypertension and slight anaemia, and he's been suffering from frequent nose-bleeds in the last couple of years. Liver function, lungs and white-cell count are normal. I've done an abdominal ultrasound and an MRI of the thigh as well as X-rays, but I'm waiting on the results of other blood tests to see if they eliminate certain other possibilities.'

Nick had obviously been very thorough. This must be an unusual case or he wouldn't have brought her in on it, and she was glad that he respected her enough to ask for her opinion.

Katie gave the boy a smile. 'Hello, Matt. I'm Dr

Logan. I'm sorry you're having problems with your thigh. That must be really uncomfortable.'

He nodded. 'I had it once before, when I was ten, but it went away. This is a lot worse.'

'Oh, dear.' She sent him a sympathetic glance. 'We'll have to find out what's wrong and put it right, then, won't we?' She studied his chart for a moment or two and then asked, 'Would it be all right if I examine you, Matt?'

'It's okay.'

Katie was as gentle as she could be, taking her time to assess the boy's condition. When she had finished she asked a few general questions about his symptoms.

'Has the swelling in his abdomen come on recently?' she said, looking at his mother.

Mrs Goren shook her head. 'It started just over two years ago. He says it isn't painful. To be honest, we didn't think anything of it at first—we just thought he was putting on a bit of weight around his tum.'

Katie nodded and glanced at the results of the ul-trasound scan on the computer monitor. 'The spleen is definitely enlarged,' she said in a low voice, looking at Nick.

'Take a look at the radiographs and MRI films,' he suggested. 'It looks to me as though there's a patchy sclerosis in the left femoral head...and abnormalities in the bone-marrow density.'

Katie studied the films. 'That could suggest re-placement of the marrow fat by an infiltrate,' she said thoughtfully.

'That's the conclusion I came to.' Nick frowned. 'This isn't something I've ever come across before, but if my suspicions are correct it could mean subjecting the boy to more invasive tests, like a bone-marrow biopsy. I'm reluctant to do that.'

'That's understandable.' She looked over the boy's notes once more then said quietly, 'You're right—this is very rare, but given the increased erythrocyte sedimentation rate, the history of nosebleeds and two separate incidents of bone pain a year apart, I'd suggest you do a blood test for glucocerebrosidase enzyme in white blood cells.'

He pulled in a deep breath. 'So you've come to the same conclusion as me—thanks for that, Katie. I was reluctant to order specialised tests on an instinctive diagnosis, but you've picked out the associated patterns of disease and helped me to make my decision. I'll go ahead with the enzyme test.'

He turned once more to his patient and spoke to the boy's mother. 'I think we'll admit Matt to hospital overnight so that we can keep him under observation and try to reduce the inflammation in his thigh. I'll arrange for a nurse to wheel him up to the ward—I'll go and organise that now—and then, once he's settled, I'll order another blood test to check for an enzyme deficiency. The sample will have to be sent off to a specialised centre for testing, but as soon as we have the results, in maybe a week's time, I'll be able to tell you more about what's going on.'

He looked at Matt. 'In the meantime, you have to rest…so that means lots of boring things like playing games on your portable computer and watching videos or TV.' He gave an exaggerated wince, and the boy laughed. 'We'll give you some tablets to take away the pain and bring your fever down,' Nick added. 'Once the leg starts to feel more comfortable, you should be up and about again—I'm hoping that will be fairly soon.'

A few minutes later, Katie said goodbye to the boy and his mother and made her way to the door. Nick excused himself and went with her, leaving the two of them to talk about Matt's hospital stay.

'Would you let me know how he goes on?' she asked, and he nodded.

'Of course.' He smiled. 'I knew I could rely on you to pinpoint the essentials,' he said as they went out into the corridor. 'You may not have been here long, but your reputation for being an excellent doctor is already hailed throughout Paediatrics and Emergency.'

'Is it?' Katie was startled. 'I'm pleased about that, of course, but I'm just doing my job, the same as everyone else.' She sent him a fleeting glance. 'Anyway, you do pretty well yourself. I thought you were brilliant with my father the other day. He hates fuss and feeling as though he's putting people out, but you handled him perfectly and you had him feeling better in very quick time. I was impressed.'

He smiled. 'We aim to please.' Then his expression sobered and he asked, 'How is Jack? Is he coping all right with his new medication?'

She nodded. 'On the whole, it's been working well, but I think he had a bit of a setback earlier today. He wasn't feeling too good first thing, apparently.'

Katie recalled the phone conversation she'd had with her father that morning. She'd sensed he'd been holding something back, but, then, he probably kept a good deal of his thoughts hidden from her. He wouldn't want her to know the full extent of his disability, and that sad-dened her. He was her father, and yet there was so much that they kept hidden from one another. How could she confide her uncertainties, and how could he share his problems with her, if no bond had built up between them over the years?

'He didn't sound quite right, and I could hear the breath rasping in his lungs, but he wouldn't admit to anything more than being a bit under the weather.' She frowned. 'I know he's using his oxygen every night, and sometimes in the daytime, too, and he seems more frail every time I see him. Of course, he never tells me any of his problems. He hates being vulnerable, and it's difficult for me to reach through to him sometimes.'

'Yes, I wondered about that.' Nick sent her an oblique glance. 'Are you and he getting on all right? I know it must be difficult for you. At the hospital the other day it was fairly obvious you and he still had a lot of issues to resolve.'

She wondered how much of their conversation he had overheard. 'That's true enough.' She frowned. 'To be honest, I don't know how I feel. I've made a real effort to break down the barriers between us lately, and I think it's beginning to pay off. I've definitely grown closer to him over these last few weeks.' Even so, doubt clouded her eyes.

'Learning to forgive must be the hardest thing of all.' Nick's gaze trailed over her features, lingering on the vulnerable curve of her mouth. 'You've had to come to terms with two betrayals, haven't you…your ex's and your father's? That's why you have so much trouble contemplating any new relationship.'

'I suppose so.' She pressed her teeth into the fullness of her lower lip. 'I hope I'm succeeding with both of those. At least with James I'm beginning to see that there were already cracks in our relationship. Maybe I was too ambitious, too set on a career path...whereas James was more easygoing, taking life as it came. I'm wondering if he simply wasn't the type to settle down. He had a child, but he didn't have much contact with him.'

'Much like your father.' Nick's expression was sombre. 'No wonder your ex's weakness hit you so hard. Your father had done exactly the same thing...followed his own path and then abandoned you.'

'Yes.' She was silent for a moment, mulling things over. Could any man be trusted? Could Nick? Not according to her father.

She frowned. 'Where my father's concerned, I still don't really understand what goes on in his head. He treats me as though he's very fond of me and has my welfare at heart...but after all those years of little or no contact it takes a bit of getting used to, to believe that he cares.' And yet only yesterday he had told her how proud he was of her, how much it pleased him that his daughter was a doctor, working to save lives. 'I needed to tell you that before I pass on,' he'd said, and she'd put her arms around him and given him a hug.

'Oh, Dad, please don't say that,' she'd implored him, her throat suddenly choked up. 'Please don't talk about passing on. I'm only just getting to know you.'

He'd smiled. 'What'll be will be.'

Nick's brooding gaze rested on her, as though he sensed something of her troubled thoughts. 'I'm sure he cares very deeply for you...but unhappily something went wrong and he didn't feel able to be there for you. Perhaps distance was a problem—living out here in California meant you were so far apart that visits would be infrequent, and he might have thought it would be less painful for you if he didn't visit at all. You would be able to settle to life without him, rather than be hurt all over again every time he went away.'

'Then again,' she pointed out, 'he could have chosen to stay in England. What was more important…his family or the job?'

He seemed to hesitate. 'That's something you must ask him yourself. I can't answer that one for you. But knowing him, I'm sure he had his reasons.'

'Did he? I've no idea what they were. All I know is that he condemned us—me and my mother—to a lonely life.' Her expression was bleak. 'Some people may like being an only child, but I wasn't one of them. I always felt there should be something more.'

He was solemn for a moment, his lips parting as though he was about to say something, but apparently he thought better of it. He laid a hand lightly on her shoulder. 'I'm sure it will all come right for you in the end, Katie. You've taken a huge step, coming out here, and you're making great headway. Just give it a little more time.'

He glanced at his watch. 'I'm off duty in a couple of hours. I'll come and pick you up from the apartment and we'll drive over to the vineyard. Perhaps that will cheer you up.'

She nodded. 'Okay. I'll be waiting.' A day or so had passed since he'd made the suggestion, and already she was beginning to regret agreeing to it. What had happened to her plan to avoid him at all costs, to steer clear of getting involved with him in any way? Working with him was proving to be a hazard in itself. It seemed that he was there at every turn…and it was impossible for her to get him out of her head.

She was beginning to realise that there was so much more to him than she had at first imagined. He was caring and perceptive and even though that made her want to get to know him a whole lot better, she was desperately afraid of the consequences. Little by little, though, he was drawing her into his electric force field and she was powerless to resist.

The vineyard, when they arrived there some time later, was bathed in late-afternoon sunlight. Nick helped her out of the passenger seat of his gleaming silver saloon and waited as she stepped out onto the wide, sweeping drive. Katie looked around. She couldn't explain it, even to herself, but just the simple fact that he was there beside her made the breath catch in her throat and in spite of herself filled her with a kind of delicious expectation. He was wearing casual clothes, a deep navy shirt, open at the neck, teamed with dark trousers, and just looking at him made her heart skip a beat.

'Let me show you round the place,' he said. 'From a high point in the gardens you can see for miles around.' He slipped an arm around her waist, his hand coming to rest on the curve of her hip in a gentle act of possession that brought heat surging throughout her body. 'I'm sure you'll love it out here,' he murmured. 'We have a beautiful day for it…the sun's shining and the vines are heavy with grapes.'

She nodded, and tried not to think about that casual touch that was so much like a caress. It only fogged her brain and left her confused and distracted.

He led the way through the house, a pretty French

château-style building that had steeply pitched roofs and round towers with turrets. Painted white, it was a gem set in the middle of the Carmel Valley, and Katie fell in love with it on sight.

The gardens were exquisitely landscaped, with trees and shrubs in full bloom so that there was a mass of colour all around. Nestled among the various arbours and flowering trees there was an elevated hardwood deck, and Nick started to head towards it.

'From up here on the deck you can see the vineyard in all its glory. It's a great vantage point,' he said, mounting the wooden stairs and walking over to the balustrade.

Katie followed him and turned to gaze at the distant Carmel Valley Mountains. 'I didn't realise that you had so much land,' she murmured. 'Are all those vines yours, or do those slopes belong to another vineyard...my father's, perhaps?'

Nick followed the direction of her gaze. 'They're ours. Your father's land is a little further to the west. We've terraced the slopes here in order to grow certain types of grapes, and then we have more vines spread along the valley floor. We're incredibly lucky in this area because there's such a long season. The grapes ripen slowly and that helps to intensify the flavour.'

She nodded, trying to take it all in. In the far distance, the verdant slopes of the ever-present Santa Lucia range added to the sense of lush, rich farmland all around. 'It looks heavenly,' she murmured, 'like an Eden where everything is in harmony and the fruit is bursting off the vines.'

He smiled. 'At least, that's how we hope it will be. A good year will produce a premium vintage, but we can't rely on that. If we get too much rain at the wrong time it can cause all kinds of problems, like mould, rot or mildew. Then again, the weather one season can be too hot and another too cool. It all helps to produce a variety of flavours and different qualities of wine.'

'So you can't simply sit back and leave things to nature?'

He laughed. 'I wish! But, no, definitely not…we have to take steps to compensate for adverse conditions.' He laid an arm around her, his hand splaying out over her shoulder and sending a thrill of heat to course through her veins. 'Over the years my family has put a huge amount of effort into building up a reputation for producing quality wines…and it all came about because of my great-great-grandfather's drive and ambition.'

She was thoughtful for a moment. 'He certainly managed to pick out a piece of prime land. He must have been an astute man—and I dare say a wealthy one, too.'

Nick shook his head. 'His family were immigrants, dirt poor, and they had to scrape a living for themselves. They came out here hoping for a better life, but it was a struggle, and I think Joseph, my great-great-grandfather, made up his mind that he would carve a path for himself, come what may. He worked at all kinds of jobs, day and night, determined to earn as much money as possible. He was thrifty, too, and put aside a good part of his earnings until, after about fifteen years or so, he had saved enough money to buy this vineyard.'

'That was a huge accomplishment.'

He nodded. 'It was. But the hardest bit was turning the vineyard around. When he first took it over they were producing inexpensive table wines, but Joseph had other ideas. He had a certain vision and he wanted to make big changes. Quality was everything to him and even though people told him he was making a big mistake, he went ahead with his plans to produce grapes that would provide superior wines. Then he had to convince the buyers that this was a product they wanted, and it all took tremendous hard work and a lot of money.'

He frowned. 'Over the years, when wine consumption declined and harvests were poor, the vineyard suffered losses that could have ruined everything for us. That's why my grandfather had to sell off a third of the land… the piece that Jack owns now. He needed the money to go on running things in keeping with Joseph's ideals.'

'And now you want it back,' Katie said flatly. 'That's why you've been asking my father to sign papers that will turn the ownership over to you once more.' She looked at him directly. 'He should have his solicitor look them over before he does anything, shouldn't he? I think I should get in touch with the law firm that deals with his affairs.' It was a subtle warning, designed to let him know that she wasn't going to stand by and see her father put under pressure. 'Only, like I said before, I don't think he's in any fit state to deal with these kinds of problems just now, do you?'

Her expression was faintly belligerent, her jaw tilted, and Nick's gaze flicked over her, taking it all in. 'I was just telling you the history of the place, that's all,' he said in an even tone. 'I don't want to get into an argument with you.'

She backed down a little. After all, she was on his territory, she was a guest here, and this was perhaps the wrong time and place to thrash out their differences.

'I'm just concerned for my father,' she said.

'I know that, and I respect you for it.' He studied

her thoughtfully. 'But if you really care about him, you would probably do well to persuade him that his life would be easier if he were to offload the worries of the business onto us. That way he could relax and enjoy his remaining years.'

She stiffened. 'I think you're mistaken if you believe I'll do your deal for you.' She sent him a flinty stare. 'I haven't had many weeks to get to know him, but it's been long enough for me to begin to care what happens to him. I didn't know what it was to have a father until now, and I've started to realise that it's something precious. I never imagined I would feel this way, about him or his land—so I'm not likely to suggest that he changes anything.'

She threw him a quick glance. 'I expect you're equally protective of your parents—more so, in fact.'

He nodded. 'I'm not criticising you in any way. It's natural that you should want to protect Jack's interests… but I'm sure he's astute enough to recognise a good deal when he sees one, and ours is far above anything he would get on the open market. Instead of trying to shield him, you could show him that it's the sensible route to follow.'

'I don't think so. I think you and your father need to back off.' She hesitated as a thought struck her. 'I don't believe you've ever mentioned your mother…'

'No.' His eyes were briefly troubled. 'She passed away some years ago…it was a virus, a nasty one that attacked her heart. The doctors did everything they could, but it wasn't enough to save her. I think she was already weak from a chest infection that laid her low.' He looked at Katie. 'I loved her dearly. She was a wonderful woman.'

'I'm sorry.' Katie pressed her lips together in a moment of regret. 'That must have been hard for all of you—your brother and your father.'

He nodded. 'Alex—my brother—was in Canada when he heard she was ill, but he came back as soon as he found out. At least we were all able to be with her at the end, and that makes it a little easier for us to bear.'

He moved away from the deck rail, becoming brisk and ready for action as though he wanted to shake off such sombre thoughts. 'Shall we go over to the winery? I said I'd take you on a tour after all.'

'Yes, I think maybe we should.' She followed him down the steps, saying, 'I was expecting some of your family to be here today—your father, maybe, or your brother.'

He shook his head. 'My father had to go into town, and Alex is in Los Angeles on business. I told him all about you, and I know he wants to meet you.'

Katie wasn't sure how to respond to that. Why would he have spoken to his brother about her? Unless, of course, he'd simply confided in his brother that a new girl had wandered in on his horizon…but perhaps she was misjudging him. It could be that her father was the factor in all this. The Bellinis were strongly allied to him through their business dealings, and it was probably only natural that they would be interested in the fact that he had a daughter—one that he had kept secret for a good many years.

They walked along a path leading from the house towards a collection of buildings some five hundred yards away. Nick pointed out a large stone-built complex where the grapes were processed, and then indicated another outbuilding where the offices and labs were housed. 'I'll show you around there later on,' he said, moving on.

She nodded. 'I know next to nothing about wine-making, I'm afraid.'

'You're not alone in that,' he murmured. He paused by a heavy wooden door set into a stone arch. 'Through here is the entrance to the cellar,' he told her. 'It has walls that are some fifteen inches thick, and it's a cool, well-ventilated environment, essential for producing good wine.'

The wine-tasting room was in a building set a little apart from these processing areas. The outer walls were painted in a soft sunshine yellow, and there were tubs of flowers and hanging baskets facing out on to the court-yard, giving it a mellow, cottage-style appearance.

'This is so pretty,' Katie said, glancing at the winery and looking back at the chateau in the distance. 'Your father must be really pleased to live in such an idyllic place.'

'I'm sure he is. I know I loved it. I was brought up here, and it was a wonderful childhood.' He looked around. 'It might be a good idea to sample the wines out here. Perhaps a table in the shade would be best.' He indicated a table in a far corner that was bordered by diamond-patterned trellises on two sides.

'Come and make yourself comfortable,' he said, hold-ing out a seat for her, 'while I go and fetch the wines.'

He returned a moment later, bearing a tray. 'We'll try a Burgundy-style Pinot Noir first of all. It's our pride and joy, the best vintage yet. See what you think of it. It's made from black grapes that grow on the cooler slopes.'

Once she was settled, he handed her a glass filled

with dark red wine, and she took a sip. It was rich and smooth, with a hint of spice and an aftertaste of black cherry plum. Katie savoured it, letting it roll over her tongue before she swallowed it. 'I can see why you're excited about this,' she said. 'I'm not a wine buff, but I do know what I like, and this is delicious.'

Nick said quietly, 'Joseph Bellini would have been proud.' He turned to Katie. 'This is what his hard work was all about, and nowadays we do our level best to live up to his vision. As well as this special wine, we produce our own Cabernet Sauvignon. It's stored in barrels made of French oak and allowed to mature over many years. The oak helps to smooth out the harsh tannins and introduces softer, wood tannins.'

Katie nodded and tasted the wine once more. 'Don't you have a problem if my father's vineyard produces similar wines? Doesn't that put you in direct competition with one another?'

He shook his head. 'Your father concentrates on Chardonnay. He had a really good season last year, and the result should be a superb wine.' He picked out another bottle. 'This is one of his Chardonnays,' he said, pouring white wine into a glass and handing it to her. 'Try it. I think you'll like it. It's full of fruit flavours—like pear, apple and melon.'

Katie sipped the wine and tried to forget for the moment that Nick and his family were doing their level best to pull her father's business out from under his feet. How could she be drawn to a man who would do that? He was the enemy and yet she was calmly sipping wine with him and enjoying the comfort of his home. She felt like a traitor.

She would simply have to be on her guard and watch

out for Jack's interests whenever possible, she decided. Maybe she would carry out her threat and get in touch with the law firm that dealt with his business affairs. The Garcias were in the phone book, and a straightforward call might do the trick. They could advise her what to do and monitor her father's dealings at the same time.

'Mmm.' She nodded. 'This is lovely.' She raised her glass to him and then looked at the tray of wines. 'I see you have at least a dozen bottles on the trolley,' she said quietly. 'At this rate I shall be tipsy before dinner.'

Nick smiled and answered under his breath, 'I think I'd quite like to see that.' Then he pulled a wry face. 'I do have a secret stash of crackers and cheese hidden away, designed to soak up the alcohol, once we've had a taster. It's a pity that we have to eat them,' he added, his voice low and husky. 'With your senses blurred, I might have been able to persuade you that I'm everything you ever wanted in a man.' His expression was mournful, and Katie stifled a laugh.

'Give it up,' she murmured. 'I wouldn't want your hopes to be dashed.'

They tasted several more wines, including the Merlot, which her father seemed to favour most of all. It was another red wine, rich and fruity with notes of currant and cherry.

Katie was glad of the savoury biscuits and the cheese platter that Nick brought out a short time later. She had missed lunch and she was beginning to feel more than a little heady. Alongside the various cheeses, there were pizza slices and *bruschetta*—slices of toasted bread topped with *prosciutto* and tomato. He had provided a selection of nuts, too, served with slices of dried apricot.

'This has been such a great experience,' she told him. 'I've never been to a wine tasting before, and to be here surrounded by greenery and row on row of vineyard slopes has been wonderful.'

'I'm glad you've enjoyed it,' he said, giving her an appreciative smile. 'Perhaps we should go along and have a look at the processing complex, before the wine goes right to your head. You're looking a trifle flushed, and it might help if you were to stretch your legs for a bit.'

'Okay.'

He helped her to her feet, and they strolled slowly over to the stone-built production plant. Nick explained some of the processes involved—the pressing of the grapes, the addition of yeast and the many checks that were done to test each stage of the fermentation process. In each separate room there were photos and clear text descriptions on the walls to enable visitors to understand what went on there. There were photos, too, of Joseph Bellini, his son Sebastian, Nick's grandfather, Thomas, and finally Robert and his two sons. Katie stared at them in wonder. They all had the same rugged good looks, the strong bone structure, and that dark, Italian machismo.

'I had no idea such a lot of effort went into producing a bottle of wine,' she told Nick a while later as they stood by the window in the scrupulously clean barn where the grapes were poured into a giant hopper. The building's double doors were open to allow a cooling drift of air into the room. 'It must be tremendously satisfying to overcome all the hazards of production and finally taste the result—and discover that it's perfection.'

'It is. Wine-making is in our blood. It has become a part of us, much as the hills and valleys all around have become our home. I wouldn't want to be anywhere else than this small corner of the world.' He gave a crooked smile. 'My brother chose to travel, to go from place to place marketing our wines, but that wouldn't do for me. My roots are here. I love this valley and my beach house. I'm very content.'

'I imagine you are.' She gazed out of the window at the surrounding hills and then looked back at him. 'You must be very proud of your ancestors...all the dedication, strength of mind and sheer stamina that has gone into making the business what it is now. No wonder you're such a fit-looking family—what I've seen of it so far. It must be in the genes.'

He leaned against a guard rail, turning to face her full on, his dark eyes glinting. 'Fit is good, isn't it?' He slightly raised dark brows. 'Does this mean you're beginning to alter your opinion of me?' He reached for her in a leisurely fashion, his hands at the base of her spine, drawing her to him and holding her lightly within the circle of his arms. 'Perhaps there's still hope I could persuade you that I'm the sort of man you could go for?'

She laughed softly. 'There's always hope, I suppose.' She looked at him from under her lashes. 'But I wouldn't get too carried away if I were you.'

'A good thing you're not me, then,' he murmured huskily, 'because I have entirely different ideas on that score. Carried away sounds just about right to me.

Carried away is a chink in the armour, and definitely something I'd like to explore a little further.'

He came towards her, his arms tightening around her waist, and as his head lowered she finally began to realise his intention. He was going to kiss her, and even though, way down in the depths of her mind, she knew she really ought to be doing something to stop him, she did nothing at all. And as his lips brushed hers in a touch that was as light as the drift of silk over her skin, she discovered the last thing on earth she wanted was to pull away.

Just the opposite, in fact. Instead, she wanted to lean into him, to revel in his warm embrace, and delight in the strength of those muscular thighs that were pressuring her softly against the cool, steel wall of the hopper. And he must have known what she wanted because he drew her ever closer until her breasts were softly crushed against the wall of his chest and she could feel the heavy thud of his heartbeat marching in time with her own.

He kissed her, tenderly at first and then with rising passion, so that his breathing became ragged and his hands began to smooth over her curves.

Katie was lost in a haze of fevered pleasure. The sun was bright in an azure sky, and for a moment or two time seemed to stand still. There was only the sensual glide of his lips as they slowly explored the contours of her face, her throat and the creamy expanse of her shoulder, laid bare by the thin straps of the cotton top she wore. And with each lingering kiss her senses soared in response.

It was all so exhilarating, so perfect, and nothing like anything she had ever experienced before. What was it about him that made her feel this way? Did he have some kind of magical touch? If so, she wanted more, much more.

Only, as his lips began to slide lower, drifting into unsafe territory, alarm bells started to ring inside her. He gently nudged aside the delicate cotton strap and ventured even further into the danger zone, trailing soft kisses over the rounded swell of her breasts and leading her to a heady, disturbing place where feeling and emotion were all, and logical thought was banished.

Even so, a tiny sliver of common sense began to filter through the mist that spread, unbidden, through her brain. Perhaps it was the swish of sprinklers being started up on the lawns outside that alerted her, or maybe it was the soft flap of a bird's wings that dragged her attention back to the reality of what was happening. What was she thinking? How could she have let this happen?

She struggled to get herself together. Wasn't Nick the man who avoided commitment? Wasn't he the one who was trying to persuade her father to sign away his land?

And here she was, betraying every instinct she possessed by falling into his arms at the first opportunity. She was a fool. She ought to have known better.

'Are you all right?' Nick lifted his head, depriving her of that heavenly, forbidden contact, and she tried to answer, but no words came. 'Have I done something wrong?' His voice was a soft murmur against her cheek.

'No... I... Yes...' She tried to ease herself away from him, her hands flattening against his chest as though she would put an end to his kisses. Why, then, did she feel the urge to stroke the velvet-covered wall of his rib cage and let her fingers explore the broad expanse of his shoulders? His muscles were firm and supple, inviting her to touch him and savour the moment.

Truly, she was a basket case—a woman at the mercy of her hormones and not to be trusted with the slightest task. 'I don't think I'm ready for this,' she said huskily. 'I shouldn't have let things get this far.'

'Are you quite sure about that?' His hands caressed her, and his tone was soft and coaxing, inviting her to drift back into the shelter of his arms once more. 'Life could be so much sweeter if only you'd allow yourself to taste it.'

She pulled in a shaky breath, willing herself to resist temptation. 'I'm sure...absolutely sure.' Even as she said it she wondered if she was trying to convince him or herself. She straightened and took a step away from him. 'I don't know how you manage to do this to me,' she said huskily, her gaze troubled. 'I need to feel good about myself, and none of this is helping. I'm very confused. I need time to think.'

'Okay.' He gave a soft, ragged sigh and moved to lay his forehead gently against hers. 'But I can't help thinking that you'd do better to throw caution to the wind. Life isn't easy. It's full of what-ifs and might-have-beens, and if you thought hard about all of them you might never experience the good side of things. I know you've been hurt, but sometimes you have to get back into the fray if you're to have another chance of happiness. Sometimes you simply have to go with your instinct and trust in people.'

Slowly, he released her, and then stood with his hands

to either side of him on the guard rail, so that she finally began to breathe a little easier.

He straightened. 'I'll walk you back to the courtyard.' He gave a crooked smile. 'You'll be safe there.'

CHAPTER SIX

KATIE placed the consultant's letter back in her tray and tried to steer her thoughts towards work. 'Good news there, at least,' she told Carla, the desk clerk, indicating the sheet of headed notepaper. 'My young patient who was rushed to hospital from here a few weeks ago is back home and on the mend.'

'The child with kidney problems? I remember his mother was so upset.' Carla gave a relieved smile. 'It's good to know he's pulled through all right. I've been worrying about him…about the poor boy with the head injury, too.'

Katie nodded. 'Me, too. Last I heard, they were thinking about moving him from the intensive care unit. I was hoping I might find time to ring and check up on him some time today, but the time has simply rushed by.' She frowned, straightening up and easing the slight ache in her back. Earlier today she had rung her father to find out how he was doing, but things weren't good, and that was playing on her mind. His nurse, Steve, was worried about his condition.

She dragged her mind back to work. 'Do I have any more patients to see this afternoon? There's nothing on my list and the waiting room's empty.'

Carla glanced at her screen once more. 'No, but there was a message from Dr Bellini. He said Matthew Goren was coming in to hospital as an outpatient today. He thought you might like to be in on the consultation with him. His appointment's scheduled for four o'clock—that gives you a quarter of an hour to get over there.'

'Right...thanks, Carla. I'd better run.'

She hurried over to the emergency department. She wasn't at all sure how she was going to cope with seeing Nick again—his scorching kisses had seared a memory into her brain that would last for all time. It made her feel hot and bothered even now, just thinking about it. And she had also been mulling over his words of advice... 'Sometimes you have to go with your instinct and trust in people.' Could she do that? Was she ready to put the past behind her and accept that she might be able to find happiness in his arms?

She went along the corridor in search of his room.

'Katie, I'm glad you could make it.' Nick's voice was deep and warm, smooth like honey drizzled over cara- melised pears. He gave her a quick smile and invited her into his office. 'I thought you might like to be in on this one. The lab results are back, and this is the last appointment of the day so there will be time to break the news to the boy and his mother without having to rush things.'

'Break the news—it's what we thought, then?'

He nodded. 'Gaucher's disease. Fortunately, even though it's rare, there are treatments for it, so it isn't as bad as it might have been some years ago. And Matt has the mildest form of the disease, so that's another point in his favour.'

He accessed the boy's notes on his computer, and they

both took time to sift through the various test results and read the letter from the consultant. When the clerk paged them a few minutes later, they were both ready to receive mother and son with smiles of greeting.

'I know you're anxious to hear the results of the tests,' Nick told them after he had made some general enquiries about the boy's state of health. 'As you know, I was concerned because Matt's spleen appeared to be enlarged and because he's been having pain in his joints. We discovered there was also some slight enlargement of the liver.'

Mrs Goren nodded. 'You took some blood for testing, and he had an MRI scan.'

'That's right.' Nick brought up the film of the scan on his computer monitor and turned to Katie. 'Do you want to explain the results?' he asked.

Katie nodded, and looked at the boy. He was a thin child, slightly underweight, with cropped brown hair that gave him an elfin look. He was looking at her now with large eyes and a faintly worried expression.

'What we discovered,' she said, 'was that you have a fatty substance in your liver and spleen. It shouldn't be there, and so we needed to find out what was going on inside you that would have caused it.'

Matt nodded, but looked puzzled and, picking up on that Katie said quickly, 'I want you to feel free to ask me questions at any time, Matt. If there's anything you don't understand, or anything you'd like to say, just go ahead.'

He frowned. 'Have you found out what caused it? Is it something I've done? The boys at school tease me.'

Katie gave him a sympathetic smile. 'No, it's nothing that you've done, and I'm sorry that you're being teased.

Perhaps when you explain to the boys what's wrong, they'll understand a bit better and stop making fun of you.'

She glanced at his mother. 'Matt has a condition called Gaucher's disease. Basically, it means that he was born without an enzyme that breaks down a substance called glucocerebroside.' She turned to Matt. 'Because you don't have this enzyme in your body, the fatty substance isn't broken down and has to find somewhere to go. Unfortunately, when it finds a home in places like your liver, your spleen or even your bones, for example, it stops those parts of you from working properly. That's why you've been having pain in your thigh, and it's the reason for you being tired all the while.'

'You're saying he was born with it?' His mother was frowning. 'Does that mean it's a hereditary disease?'

Mrs Goren's gaze flew in alarm from Katie to Nick, and Nick answered quietly, 'That's right. You and your husband may not suffer from the disease, but it's possible that either one or both of you may be a carrier. It can go back through generations, although there may not be anyone in the family that you know of directly who has the disease.'

All at once Mrs Goren looked close to tears and Katie hurried on to say, 'The *good* news is that we do have treatment for it.' She smiled at Matt. 'There's something called enzyme replacement therapy, which helps to break down this fatty substance and should soon start to improve things for you.'

Matt's brow cleared, and his mother dabbed at her eyes with a tissue and did her best to pull herself together. She looked at Nick. 'Can we start him on this treatment straight away?'

He responded cautiously. 'I can arrange an appointment for him at the hospital. The answer isn't as simple as taking a tablet, I'm afraid, but what happens is that Matt will be given an infusion—it takes about an hour to administer, and the treatment is given once a fortnight. He'll need to stay with the treatment for life, until such time as science comes up with a better answer. It's a rare disease. Of course, he'll be carefully monitored on a regular basis, so that we can check how he's responding.'

Katie was silent, watching as mother and son tried to absorb what he had just told them. Nick waited, too, before gently asking if they had any questions for him. He was unfailingly patient and kind, and her respect for him grew. In fact, every time she saw him at work, she marvelled at his caring, conscientious manner.

Mrs Goren and Matt both remained quiet for a moment or two longer. Perhaps they had all the information they could handle for the time being. It was a lot to take in, but the consolation was that from now on they would receive masses of help from the clinic at the hospital...along with ongoing input from Nick and herself, of course.

'Will the treatment cause the swelling to go down?' Mrs Goren asked, and Nick nodded.

'You should see a great improvement.' He looked at Matt. 'And the pain will go away.'

After answering a few more questions, and doing what he could to put the mother's mind at ease, he said, 'Let me leave you with some reading material that I've printed out for you. I'm sure there will be things that you think of once you leave here, but I'm hoping that these papers will help answer any immediate queries...

and, of course, you can always come and see me again if you want to talk.'

Katie glanced at Nick. That was a thoughtful touch—he had gone that one step further to give his patient everything he could, and she could see that Mrs Goren was pleased.

Nick gave his attention to Matt, and said, 'The nurses and doctors at the clinic will look after you and explain anything you want to know. Next time you come to the hospital for an outpatient appointment, I'm sure you'll be feeling a whole lot better. In the meantime, keep taking the painkillers if you have any more trouble with your thigh, and get plenty of rest. Once you get started on the treatment, I'm certain you'll begin to feel much more energetic.'

Matt nodded. 'Thanks,' he said, and gave a shuddery sigh. 'I thought I had some horrible illness that was going to make me die, but it's not as bad as that, is it?'

'No, it isn't,' Nick told him with a reassuring smile, and Katie's heart went out to this child who had suffered in silence all this time. 'And if you ever have worries of any kind,' Nick added, 'please speak up. Don't keep it to yourself. Often things aren't nearly as bad as you think, and we're here to help you in any way we can.'

After they left, Nick invited Katie to stay awhile and made coffee for both of them. 'I need to write up my notes while they're fresh in my mind—but perhaps we can talk after that?'

'Okay.' She sipped her coffee and leaned back in her chair, thinking about the day's events. From a medical standpoint at work, things had gone well, but she felt uneasy somehow. There was still that niggling worry over her father's health.

She gave a faint sigh, and then stretched. What she needed right now was a complete change of scene, a trip to the beach, perhaps or maybe even a walk through the cobbled streets of the town. But that wasn't likely to happen for a while... Perhaps she ought to go and see her father, see how he was bearing up. There might be something she could do for him.

'Are you okay?' Nick asked.

Caught off guard, Katie quickly tried to collect her thoughts. She hadn't realised he'd been watching her. 'I'm fine, thanks.'

His gaze flicked over her. 'You seem...pensive. If there's something wrong, perhaps I can help?'

She shook her head. 'I was just thinking about my father—I feel that I should go over to his place to see if he's all right. I rang this morning and he was having a bad day, according to the nurse, Steve. It's a bit worrying—apparently he was talking but not making much sense.'

Nick winced. 'That happens sometimes when the blood oxygen levels are low.'

'Yes. Even so, I asked Steve to send for the doctor to see if he would prescribe a different medication. He hasn't called me yet to let me know what happened. I suppose he's been too busy, with one thing and another, or perhaps he didn't want to tie up the phone line if the doctor was likely to call.'

'That's probably the case.' He studied her thoughtfully. 'Would you like me to go with you to see him? It's never easy when someone in the family is ill, is it?'

'No, it isn't.' She might have known Nick would

understand. He had been through difficult times with his mother in the past, and it said a lot about his compassion and perception that he was offering to be by her side. 'Thank you,' she said softly. 'I'd really like it if you would be there with me.'

'We'll go as soon as I've finished up here,' he said, becoming brisk and ready for action. 'Give me five minutes.'

A feeling of relief swept over her. She didn't know why she had involved Nick in any of this, there was no accounting for her actions, and she was working purely on instinct. All at once, though, she felt that with him by her side, she could handle anything.

They went out to his car a short time later, which was in a leafy, private space in the car park. She glanced at him. Even after a day's work, he looked cool and fresh, dressed in dark trousers and crisp linen shirt that perfectly outlined his long, lean figure. His black hair glinted with iridescent lights as they walked in the sunlight, and she gazed at him for a moment or two, wondering what it was about him that stirred her blood and made her want to be with him.

He touched her hand, clasping it within his, and suddenly she felt safe, cherished, as though all was right with the world. 'I'm here for you, Katie,' he said softly. 'Any time you need me.'

Her heart swelled with joy. The truth was, he had never been anything but good towards her. He had treated her with warmth and respect, with care and attention, and he was here now, ready to be by her side at a moment's notice and support her through what promised to be a difficult time. What more could she ask?

She stood in the shade of a cypress tree, watching

him as he paused to unlock the car, and it finally hit her that she was bedazzled by him. He made her heart thump and her thoughts go haywire, and there was no knowing why it was happening. Why was she holding back? She might just as well cast her fears to one side and start living again, mightn't she?

Okay, so she had been hurt once before. Her ex had had a child by another woman and had shocked her to the core with his infidelity, but that didn't have to mean all men were of a similar nature, did it? Was she going to let that experience ruin her life for evermore?

Nick came to stand beside her, his lips curving in a faint smile, and he said softly, 'Are you feeling all right? You look different somehow.'

A faint bubble of laughter rose in her throat. 'I'm fine. I'm just so glad that you're here with me. Whatever happens, I feel as though I'll be able to cope with it, just as long as we're together.'

'That's good to know.' His voice faded on a shuddery sigh. 'I've waited a long while for you to learn to trust me, Katie. I won't let you down, I promise.'

He wrapped his arms around her and kissed her gently on the mouth. His touch was light as the drift of silk, but it sent fiery signals to every nerve ending in her body, and she wanted to cling to him, to savour that moment and make it last for ever.

Her fingers lightly stroked his arms and then moved up to tangle with the silky hair at his nape. She belonged in his arms, it felt right, as though it was the only place to be at that moment.

He kissed her again, trailing kisses over her cheek, her throat, and then with a soft, ragged sound he reluctantly dragged himself away from her.

'Wrong place,' he said in a roughened tone, as though that explained things. 'I can think of better places where I can show you how much I care.'

Katie stared at him, blankly, her lips parting, a tingle of delicious sensation still running through her from head to toe.

He sent her an oblique glance in return, his mouth twisting a little. 'Did I go too far again?' he asked. 'I hope not, because I really wanted to do that. In fact, it's on my mind every time I see you—and even sometimes when we're apart.'

She didn't answer, still lost in that haze of delirious excitement. He'd kissed her…he cared about her… All at once the world was bright and new. Was this love?

Nick pulled in a deep breath, as though to steady himself. He held open the passenger door for her and she slid dazedly into the air-conditioned comfort of his car. Then he went around to the driver's side, coming to sit beside her.

He turned the key in the ignition, starting up the car. 'I need to get my head right,' he said. 'Perhaps we should talk about everyday kind of things for a while—like work, for instance.'

She blinked and closed her mouth, trying her utmost to bring her thoughts back down to a level plane, and he went on cautiously, 'I thought you might like to know—I checked up on Darren Mayfield this afternoon.'

'You did?' She finally found her voice. 'Oh, I'm glad of that. I haven't had time to ring the unit yet today. How's he doing? I know they were thinking of moving him from Intensive Care.'

He nodded. 'That's right. I know you've been keeping tabs on his condition over the last week or so. Anyway, he's on the main ward now and he seems on course to make a full recovery. There's some weakness in his limbs apparently, but the physiotherapist is going to be working with him and he looks set to be back to normal within a few weeks.'

Her face lit up. 'Oh, that's wonderful news...the best.'

He nodded. 'I knew you'd be pleased.' He set the car in motion and turned his attention to the road, leaving her to gaze out at the passing landscape.

'You said you'd been to see your father's vineyard,' Nick remarked as he turned the car on to the valley road. 'Of course, he doesn't live on the property—his manager is the one who stays on the premises. I expect you'll have met him when you went over there.'

Katie nodded. 'Yes, I've been introduced to Toby. He seems a very friendly and approachable man. At least he was willing to answer all my naïve questions. Like I said, I've been fascinated with the whole process of growing vines and turning the fruit into wine ever since I came over here and learned what my father was doing.'

Nick frowned. 'You could always ask me anything you want to know...anytime. I'd be only too glad to tell you. We could even combine it with dinner out or supper at one of the ocean view restaurants around here, if you like. Or a stroll along the beach if that takes your fancy more.'

Her mouth curved. 'I'll definitely think about it. They all sound good to me.'

He relaxed, a look of satisfaction crossing his face. 'Wow! I think I'm actually winning for a change! Wake me up, I think I might be dreaming!'

'I seriously hope not,' she said with a laugh, 'or any minute now you'll be crashing the car into my father's gatepost.'

They had reached her father's property, a stone-built house set in a secluded area some short distance from the coastal stretch where Nick had his home. They approached it along a sweeping drive that cut through well-kept lawns, bordered in part by mature trees and flowering shrubs.

The house was a solid, rectangular building on two storeys, with the ground-floor windows placed symmetrically either side of a wide doorway.

Katie frowned as Nick drew the car to a halt. 'It looks as though my father has a visitor,' she said. 'I don't recognise that four by four, do you?'

'It's the doctor's car. Dr Weissman—I've known him for some years now.'

'Oh, yes.' Katie collected her thoughts. 'I think I've bumped into him once or twice.' Her gaze was troubled. 'I wonder if my father's taken a turn for the worse?'

Nick was already sliding out of the car, and she hurried to join him on the gravelled forecourt. It was a fresh, warm summer's day, but the sun went behind a cloud just then and a sudden sense of foreboding rippled through her. She walked quickly towards the oak front door and rang the bell.

Libby, the housekeeper, came to answer it, looking unusually flustered. 'Oh, Katie, there you are.' She pulled open the door and ushered them inside. 'I was just about to call you,' she said, pulling at a wayward strand of soft brown hair. 'The doctor and Steve are with your father now. Jack's been having a bad time of it all day. It's his heart, I think. At least, that's what the doctor said.'

'I need to go and see him,' Katie said, a thread of unease edging her words. The feeling of dread that clutched at her midriff since she'd arrived at the house was intensifying by the minute.

'I understand how you must be feeling,' Libby answered, worry lines creasing her brow, 'but the doctor said he would come and let us know as soon as there was any news.'

Katie frowned. 'But I'm his daughter. I want to be with him. I want to know what's going on.'

The housekeeper's face seemed to crumple, and she made a helpless, fluttering gesture with her hands, as though this was all getting too much for her, and Katie said quickly, 'It will be all right, Libby, I promise. We made up our differences a while ago, my father and I… he'll want me to be there with him. I know he will.'

Libby was still fraught with indecision. 'I should have rung you earlier, I know I should, but I had to ring for an ambulance and try to contact the others and that took up so much time. It's been such an awful day, one way and another. And the ambulance still hasn't arrived.'

Katie frowned. What others? What was Libby talking about? But perhaps she had tried to phone Jack's friends, the people who knew him best…along with the doctor, of course. Katie might be his daughter, but she had only been in town for a couple of months at most.

Nick took hold of her arm, as though to add a helping hand, and she turned to him in gratitude. 'Thanks for bringing me here. It looks as though things are much more serious than I thought. Otherwise why would Dr Weissman have wanted an ambulance?'

'It does sound as though he's concerned,' Nick admitted, 'but let's wait and hear what he has to say.'

'I must go to my father,' she said again. She knew the way to Jack's room from the first time she had been there, when her father had shown her around, and despite Libby's distressed expression she made an instant decision and began to head in that direction.

Nick went with her, but as they came to the first floor and walked along the corridor, the door of her father's room opened and Steve walked out.

He stopped as soon as he saw them and pulled in a deep, calming breath. 'Katie,' he greeted her. 'I don't think you should go in there just yet. Let me talk to you for a while. Shall we find somewhere to sit down?' He glanced at Nick, and an odd look passed between them. Katie didn't understand it. Hadn't that same mysterious kind of glance occurred when she and her father had had dinner together and she'd met Nick for the first time?

She allowed Nick to lead her away, following Steve along the corridor and back down the stairs to the sitting room.

'Please, sit down, Katie.' Steve indicated a comfortable sofa and then turned to Nick. 'You, too, Nick,' he said.

Katie did as he suggested, feeling for the settee with the back of her legs and not once taking her gaze off Steve. Nick sat down beside her, and the nurse took the armchair opposite.

She was more bewildered than ever. Something was going on here and she had no idea what it could be. Right now, though, she wanted more than anything to know what was happening with her father.

'Katie,' Steve began quietly, 'I'm really sorry to be the

one to tell you this…but I'm afraid your father passed away a few minutes ago. In the end his heart simply gave out.'

'No…' Katie's mind refused to take it in. 'That can't be… I only spoke to him on the phone this morning. How can this be happening?' For all her training as a doctor, coming face to face with the death of a loved one was turning out to be every bit as difficult for her as it was for her patients. She had no idea it could be so hard to accept.

Nick put his arm around her and held her tight. 'I'm so sorry, Katie. It's a shock—in fact, it's a shock for both of us.'

Steve pressed his lips together in a fleeting moment of sadness. 'Dr Weissman did everything he could to try to resuscitate him, but in the end it was impossible. There was nothing more he could do.'

Katie was bewildered. 'I just can't take it in. I came here thinking he was just having one of those bad days. He always seemed so stoical, so determined to get the best out of life.'

'And I'm sure he did, Katie.' Nick leant his cheek against hers. 'He was over the moon because you had come out here to see him. These last few weeks he was always talking about you, saying how well you'd done for yourself.'

'Was he?' Tears began to trickle slowly down her face. 'It seems such a waste. All these years I've waited, wanting to get to know him but always holding back because I was afraid of what I might find. It took me such a long time to forgive him for walking out on my mother and me. It was such a strange sort of life…as if it was somehow off key. And now he's gone.'

He held her close, letting her weep for what might have been, and all the time he stroked her hair, comforting her just by being there for her when she needed him most.

Libby brought in a tray of tea and quietly set it down on the coffee table. 'The doctor's gone into the kitchen to fill in his forms. He's very sad. They were good friends—your father always spoke highly of him.'

Katie glanced up at Libby. The woman was ashenfaced, struggling to keep her emotions in check.

'Perhaps you should sit down and give yourself some time,' Katie suggested softly, still shaken but subdued. 'You must be as upset as the rest of us. More so, perhaps...my father told me you'd been with him for years.'

Libby put a tissue to her face. 'I have, yes, that's true.' She wrung her hands. 'I ought to go and...' She turned distractedly, as though to go out of the door, and then changed her mind and came to sit down on one of the straight-backed chairs by a polished mahogany desk. 'I don't know what to do,' she said in a broken voice.

'Don't do anything. Just sit for a while and I'll get you some tea.' Katie moved as though to go and pour a cup, but Nick gently pressured her back into the sofa.

'I'll do it,' he said. 'You stay there.'

Steve looked towards the sitting-room door while Nick poured tea and handed it around. 'I should go and have a word with the doctor,' he murmured. 'He'll need someone to see him out...and I'd better call the paramedics and tell them what's happened.'

He walked over to the door and opened it, walking out into the hallway. The sound of voices coming from there alerted Katie and made her sit up and take notice. Had the paramedics arrived already?

'We just want to talk to Libby for a minute or two,' a male voice said. 'There will be things to arrange.'

Steve said quietly, 'Perhaps it can wait for a while. Libby's in shock, as we all are. Do you want to go and talk to the doctor instead, in the kitchen?'

'Not just yet.' The sound of the man's voice drew nearer, and Katie looked across the room as the door opened. A young man walked in, followed by a slender girl who looked to be slightly older than him, about twenty-three or twenty-four years old. She was pretty, with auburn hair that fell in bright curls about her shoulders, but right now her features were taut, as though she was doing her best to hold herself together.

Katie stood up, dragging her thoughts away from all that had happened and making an effort to behave in the way that Jack would have expected. He would want her to politely greet his guests and make them welcome, even now.

'Hello,' she said, going over to them. 'I don't think we've met before, have we? I'm Katie. For a moment there I thought you were the paramedics.'

The young man shook his head. 'I think the doctor rang and told them there was no urgency.'

'Yes, that would be the sensible thing to do.' Katie studied him briefly. He had black hair and hazel eyes, and she had the impression he was struggling to keep his emotions under control, his face showing signs of stress, with dark shadows under his eyes and a gaunt, hollowed-out appearance to his cheeks.

'I'm Tom Logan,' he said, 'and this is my sister, Natasha.' He put an arm around the girl's shoulders.

'You've caught us at a bad time. I expect you've heard that our father has just died. Did you know him? Were you a friend of his?'

Katie almost reeled back in shock. She stared at him. *Their father?* Surely there had to be some mistake? She felt as though all the breath had been knocked out of her and for a moment or two she simply stood there and tried to absorb his words.

'I didn't realise...' she began after a while, but broke off. There couldn't be any mistake, could there? *Logan*, he had said. How much clearer could he have made it?

'Are you all right?' Tom was frowning, looking perplexed, and his sister pulled in a shaky breath and tried to show her concern, too.

It wasn't fitting that she should be here, Katie decided suddenly. These were Jack's children, and they had the right to grieve in peace. She had to get out of here. 'Yes, I...' She swallowed hard. 'I have to go... I need to get some air...' This wasn't the time or the place to explain who she was and where she had come from, was it? They'd obviously had no idea that she existed before this.

She swivelled round, desperate to get out of there, away from all these people. All at once she felt as though she was part of a topsy-turvy world where nothing made sense any more. She needed to be alone, to try to take it all in.

'Katie's upset,' she heard Nick saying. 'This has all been a bit too much for her. Excuse us, please. I think I'd better take her home.'

Katie was already out of the front door, standing on the drive, when she realised that she didn't have her own car there. But perhaps that was just as well. She was probably in no state to drive.

Was it too far away for her to walk home? She could always get a taxi, couldn't she? But for now she just needed to keep moving, to get away from there, to get her head straight.

'Katie, wait, please.' Nick dropped into step beside her.

'Why would I do that?' She shot the words at him through gritted teeth. 'I really don't have anything to say to you.' She kept on walking. Hadn't he known all along?

'But we need to talk this through,' he said. 'You've had a shock—a double shock, given what's happened to Jack.'

'Yes, I've had a shock—and whose fault is that, precisely?' The words came out flint sharp. 'Did you really think you could hide it from me for ever? Why would you want to do that?' She clamped her lips together. 'No, don't answer that. I don't want to hear it. You colluded with him, let me go on thinking I was the daughter he loved and cared about, when all the time he…' She couldn't get the words out. Her anger was rising in a tide of blood that rushed to her head. It made her feel dizzy, and it thumped inside her skull like the stroke of a relentless mallet.

'It wasn't the way you think…believe me…'

'Believe you?' She gave a harsh laugh. 'Why should I believe you?' She looked at him, her green eyes glinting with barely suppressed fury. 'Why should I listen to anything you have to say? I was foolish enough to think that you had some integrity, that you were different to the others…that you could be honest with me. Well, I was wrong.' She was still walking, her footsteps taking her out through the large wrought-iron gates, flanked on either side by stone-built gateposts.

'Katie, this is madness. At least stop and talk to me. Let me explain.'

'There's nothing to explain, is there? I know exactly how it went. You knew all along that my father had another family, a family he didn't want me to know about… or my mother, for that matter. How old is Natasha, do you imagine? Twenty-four? That means she was born while he was still married to my mother. How do you think I feel about that? Can you imagine? And yet I still would have wanted to know that they existed. Don't you think I had a right to know?'

'Of course you did. And he would have told you, given time. It's just that he wanted to pick his moment. You were getting along so well together. He didn't want to spoil that.'

He frowned. 'Katie, you've only just discovered that he's passed on. You're bound to be upset and not thinking clearly about things. You're emotional and over-wrought, and you should give yourself time to get used to the idea that he's gone before you start dissecting his behaviour and giving yourself grief over it. You'll have a much more balanced outlook in a day or so's time.'

'Will I? I think I have a pretty firm handle on the situation right now. I might even forgive my father for his deception…after all, I've been there before. He left us back in England and eventually I managed to come to terms with what he had done. I know what kind of man he is…' her voice lowered to a whisper. 'Was.'

She stopped walking and faced him head on. 'It's you I have a problem with. You're the one who kept the pretence going. You banded together to keep me in the dark about it, about my family—my brother and sister, for heaven's sake.'

She shook her head as though to throw out all the debris of broken dreams that had gathered there. 'You knew how lonely I was through all those years after he left us,' she said, her eyes blurred with tears. 'You knew how much it hurt me to be rejected and how desperately I needed to know the reason for that. You should have told me the truth…that he had another family out here, one that he was prepared to stand by, to love and protect. It would have helped me to understand. I wouldn't have kept my hopes up that my relationship with my father could have been something more than it was.'

Her gaze locked with his. 'Instead, you let me flounder and lose my way. You made it so that I stumbled across his children at the worst possible moment. You could have stopped all that, and yet you did nothing.'

'Katie, I had to keep it from you. Jack made me promise. He wanted to tell you himself when the time was right.'

'Well, you should never have made that promise,' she told him flatly. 'Because of it, all my illusions are shattered. I thought I knew you. I thought I could trust you…but I was wrong.' She took in a shuddery breath. 'You should go back to the house, Nick. I need to be alone.'

CHAPTER SEVEN

'IF THERE'S anything at all that I can do to help you through these next few weeks, Dr Logan, please be sure to give me a call…at any time.' The lawyer handed Katie his embossed card. 'I know this must be a particularly difficult time for you.'

'Thank you.' Katie accepted the card and slipped it into her bag. She was still numb from everything that had happened over the last couple of weeks. Her father had died, the will had been read and now she had to try to pick up the pieces and go on with her life.

How was she to do that? Nick had betrayed her. The one man she'd thought she could trust had let her down, with devastating consequences. He'd once told her that she was special and that she'd shaken him to the core, and yet those had been empty words. It seemed those feelings were fragile, and he was easily diverted.

His duplicity left her feeling utterly lost and alone and she couldn't see how she was ever going to recover from this.

Even now, Nick was watching her from across the room. It was bad enough that he was there at all, but there was nothing she could do about that. She could feel his dark gaze homing in on her, piercing like a laser, but she was determined to ignore him. She wanted to avoid him at all costs. He'd known all along about Tom and Natasha, but he had said nothing. How could he have left her to find out about them that way? If he had cared anything for her, wouldn't he have told her?

'It can't have been easy for you, discovering that you had a family out here in California,' the lawyer commented.

'No,' she confessed. She'd had two long weeks to think about that awful day at her father's house, and now she was here with her half-brother and -sister, gathered together under the same roof once more, and it was every bit as unsettling now as it had been then. 'I'm finding it all a bit of a strain, I must admit. I'm still struggling to take it all in. It hadn't occurred to me that my father would leave the vineyard, the house—everything, in fact—to the three of us.' She frowned. 'I'm not sure what I expected, really…after all, I hadn't been part of his life for some twenty years.'

'The terms of the will were very precise.' His brows drew together in a dark line. 'After his second wife died, he stipulated that the property and the land should go to his children, and he named each one of you specifically. It wasn't an afterthought. He had the will drawn up several years ago. Other bequests were added later—like the monetary gifts to his housekeeper and manager.'

'And the collection of rare books that went to Nick Bellini.' That was the reason for him being there, wasn't it, on a day when she'd thought she would be safe?

He nodded. 'Jack knew that he had a special interest in them, and he wanted to thank him for his help over the years. He said Nick had always been there to advise him about matters to do with the vineyard, and lately he had looked out for him when he was ill.'

'It sounds as though you knew my father very well.' Her mouth softened. 'He must have talked to you quite a bit about these things.'

'That's true. I often had occasion to meet with him, so we got to know one another on a friendly as well as a professional basis. I had a lot of respect for your father.'

Katie's mouth made a faint downward curve. It was a pity she couldn't share that opinion. Her world had been turned upside down when she had discovered her father's secret. Now she would remember him as a weak man who hadn't had the courage to admit to his shortcomings. How much grief would he have spared his family if he had done that? Even her mother had echoed those thoughts at his funeral.

For Katie's part, she wanted to weep. What was it about her that made people treat her this way? As a child, for a long time after her father left she had felt that she was unlovable...worthless...and now those feelings of rejection and isolation were intensified.

Was there anyone she could rely on? Her ex had cheated on her, and her own father had left her so that he could be with his other family. And now Nick had hurt her deeply by keeping her in the dark about her brother and sister. If he'd cared about her at all, wouldn't he have confided in her, tried to smooth her path and let her know about something so significant as a family that was being hidden from her?

'How are you bearing up?' Nick came to join them, and the lawyer discreetly excused himself to go and talk to her new siblings. 'If there's anything I can do—'

'You could stay away,' she said, slanting him a brief, cool stare.

'I'm sorry you feel that way.' His gaze flicked over her, taking in the silky sheen of her chestnut hair, the troubled curve of her mouth, and then shifted downwards over the slender lines of her dove-grey suit. The jacket nipped in at the waist, emphasising the flare of her hips, while the slim skirt finished at the knee, showing off an expanse of silk-smooth legs. 'I was hoping by now you'd have had time to think things through... and maybe come to the conclusion that I'd acted with the best of intentions.'

'Then you'll be disappointed. I won't forgive you for holding back from me. You let me down. You betrayed my trust...my faith in you. I'd begun to think you were someone I could believe in, but it turns out you're no different from any of the other men in my life.'

His head went back at that and sparks flared in his eyes, as though she had slapped him. A moment later, though, he recovered himself and said in an even tone, 'I can see I've a lot of fences to mend. I hoped you would understand that I did what I felt was right. I had to keep my promise to your father.'

She gave an indifferent shrug. 'That's as may be. I'm not disputing that. You made your choice and you stuck by it. That's fine. Just don't expect me to agree with you. If you had any thought for my feelings at all, you would have warned me. Instead, you let me blunder on, thinking I actually had a father who loved me but who had simply made a mistake.' Her jaw clenched. 'But, of course, it turns out that *I* was the mistake. That's laughable, isn't it? The offspring who really mattered to him are standing over there, talking to his lawyer.' Her gaze was steel sharp. 'You colluded with him.' She gave an imitation of a smile. 'I must have thrown the cat among the pigeons, turning up here out of the blue.'

His mouth compressed. 'You know I'm not to blame for any of that, Katie. You're putting the sins of your father onto me. Don't you think you're mixing things up in your head just a little?'

'No, I don't. Not at all.' Her mouth tightened. 'You should have told me, and you could at the very least have persuaded my father to tell me, instead of leaving things until it was too late.'

She started to turn away from him. 'I'm going to talk to Libby for a while,' she said, 'and maybe I'll go and help myself to something from the buffet.' She threw him a warning glance. 'I hope that doesn't mean you'll feel obliged to butt in there as well.'

A muscle flicked in his jaw. 'You're mistaking concern for interference, Katie. I only want what's best for you.'

Katie's mouth twisted. 'Whatever. I don't need your help or your concern. It's way too late for that.' She walked away from him, going over to the buffet table where Libby was standing alone, looking lost. She had to get away from him.

The truth was, she still could not sort out in her mind where everything had gone wrong. He had stolen into her heart and she had glimpsed a snapshot of how wonderful her life might be with him as part of it. She had begun to care for him and those feelings lingered on, in spite of herself. It wrenched her heart to know what a fool she had been to fall for him.

Natasha came to join them a minute or so later. 'I'm just going to grab a quick bite to eat and then I'll go and fetch Sarah down from upstairs.' She bit into a cheese topped cracker, savouring it as though she hadn't eaten for hours.

Katie frowned. 'Who's Sarah?' she asked.

'Oh, of course, you don't know, do you?' Natasha smiled. 'She's my little girl. I laid her down in the cot upstairs before you arrived. Even with the excitement of a house full of people, she was ready for sleep.' She helped herself to a sandwich. 'I thought I heard her stirring a minute ago. She usually naps for a couple of hours in the afternoon, so I take my opportunities while I can.' She waved the sandwich in explanation.

'I'd no idea,' Katie said. 'You look so young, and I'd assumed you were single, like Tom.'

Natasha smiled. 'She's eighteen months old—I've been married for four years, but Greg and I separated a few months ago, so it's just Sarah and me now.' Her mouth flattened briefly. 'Not that she's any trouble. Lately, she just wants to sit quietly and play with her dolls. None of that racketing about that she used to do when she first started to walk.' She frowned, thinking about it. 'Perhaps I ought to take her to the doctor. She's definitely not as lively as she used to be…but, then, I don't want to be labelled as a fussy mother, and it could be that she's fretting over her father.' She crammed another cracker into her mouth, brushed the crumbs from her hands and hurried away. 'Must go and check on her,' she said.

Katie watched her go, feeling a little sad. There were so many things she didn't know about her newfound family. They had at least twenty-four years of catching up to do.

'We ought to get together over the next day or so,'

Tom said, coming to the table to pour himself a cup of coffee from the ceramic pot. 'There's been a lot to take in today, and the land and holdings are all a bit complex, so we really need to iron out what we're going to do.' He looked around. 'There's no use doing it here. I can't think straight in this house…too many memories. I can see Dad in my mind everywhere I go. And if today's anything to go by, there are likely to be interruptions, with visitors stopping by to pay their respects over the next week or so.'

He swallowed his drink. 'Nick has offered us the use of a conference room at his hotel. It's quiet there, and the lawyer, Antony, has said he'll come along and talk us through things in detail. I thought Wednesday would be a good day for it—you have a half-day then, don't you, Katie?'

'Um…yes, that's right.' Katie was looking at Nick, who had somehow managed to appear by Tom's side. The last thing she wanted to do was spend time at Nick's hotel. He must surely be aware of that.

His gaze meshed with hers and in that moment she knew without a doubt that he had set this up. There was a hint of satisfaction in the faint curve of his mouth. She might run, his blue eyes were telling her, but he would always be there, in her wake.

'I ran it by Natasha, and she's okay with that,' Tom said, 'so if it's all right with you, Katie, we could go ahead and make arrangements.'

She could hardly disrupt their plans for her own selfish reasons, could she? Katie flinched inwardly, but heard herself saying, 'Wednesday's fine by me,' and Nick's mouth curved.

'Juice!' A child's voice cut into their conversation,

sounding clear and sharply commanding, and Katie looked round to see Natasha crossing the room. 'Juice, Mummy.' A chubby little hand appeared from out of the blanket-wrapped bundle that Natasha was carrying, the fingers curling and uncurling as the child poked her head above the fleece and spied the jugs of orange juice on the table. Pale faced, she had a mass of auburn curls that quivered around her cheeks with her excitement at seeing the buffet table.

'There's a girl who knows exactly what she wants.' Nick laughed, glancing from the infant to Natasha. 'Would you like me to get it for you? You seem to have your hands full.'

'Would you? Thanks.' Natasha handed him the child's drinking cup. 'She's such a fussy madam, this one…and you're right, she's very clear about what she wants. She'll never settle for second best.'

'Seems to me that's a good enough way to go through life.' Nick filled the cup, pressing the lid into place before handing it to the child.

'Tanka,' Sarah said, giving him a beaming smile and sucking on the spout of the cup as though she hadn't seen a drink in twenty-four hours.

'Um…tanka?' Nick echoed, looking at Natasha for an explanation.

'I'm trying to teach her please and thank you,' Natasha answered. 'She hasn't quite got the hang of thank you yet.'

'Oh, I see.' Nick chuckled. He glanced at Sarah once more and commented softly, 'I see you made short work of that, missie. I guess sleeping made you thirsty.'

'More!' Sarah reached out and waved the cup in front of his nose, and as he gently took it from her, she lunged towards him and planted an open-mouthed kiss on his cheek, letting her face linger there as though she was testing him out for touch and taste.

'Well, that was nice,' Nick murmured with a smile, gently disentangling himself from a mound of blanket as Sarah finally retreated. 'It's good to be appreciated.'

Watching the two of them brought a lump to Katie's throat. Nick seemed perfectly at home with the child's gloriously uninhibited behaviour. Seeing him relate to her, she could almost imagine him as a father—he would be a natural from the looks of things.

Her heart flipped over, even as her mind veered away from that startling thought. Over the last few years she had wondered what it would be like to have a family of her own, but she felt totally ill equipped for the role. Perhaps with the right man by her side, it would be different. She glanced at Nick once more, this time with wistfulness in her gaze. Why did all her hopes and dreams come to nothing? First her ex, and then her relationship with her father, and now Nick had let her down. What was wrong with her that these things kept happening? Why couldn't she be happy?

Nick caught her glance, sending her a thoughtful look in return, and she quickly turned away.

'Do you have any nieces or nephews back in England?' Tom was saying, and she came out of her reverie with a start. 'You haven't told us much about yourself up to now.'

'Uh—no, I don't, I'm afraid.' She smiled briefly. 'I'm an only child—or at least I thought I was until now. I wish I'd known about you and Natasha before this. I would have liked to be part of a family—or to feel that I was, anyway. It makes me regret that I didn't have the confidence to come out here earlier. I feel I've missed out on so much.' What must it be like to know the intimacy and joy that came from having young people around, from sharing a household with siblings?

'Perhaps that's why you chose to work with children,' Nick suggested, his glance moving over her, almost as though he had read her thoughts. 'That way you get to have the contact with youngsters that was missing from your life. It isn't the same, I know, but it must help in some way.'

He was perceptive, she had to give him that...far more perceptive than any man she'd known up to now. 'I expect you're right,' she murmured. 'I hadn't thought about it that way.'

'It must be very fulfilling work, being a paediatrician,' Natasha commented. She set Sarah down on the floor so that she could toddle along to a corner of the room where Libby had set out a box of toys. 'We rely on doctors so much when things go wrong. I know when Sarah had a nasty virus a few weeks ago I was really worried, but it helped to talk things through with my doctor.'

She frowned. 'I don't do anything nearly so grand as you—I work in an office, part time, and Libby looks after Sarah for me while I'm away from home. I don't know what I'd do without her. The job doesn't pay very well, but I didn't want to work full time and lose out on Sarah's young years.' She grimaced. 'I suppose things will be a little easier once we've sorted out the inheritance, though everything's tied up in land and property from the sound of things...and stocks and shares.' She hesitated, thinking through what she had said. 'That sounds awful, doesn't it, thinking about the estate when we've only just lost our father?'

'I know what you mean, though,' Tom said. 'I started up my business a year ago—glass manufacture,' he added, for Katie's benefit, 'but without injecting extra capital I can't see how the company will survive for much longer.'

Katie looked from one to the other. 'Did neither of you want to follow in your father's footsteps?'

Natasha shook her head. 'It was very much his thing, you know. He didn't really involve us in it, and we didn't exactly badger him to let us know the ins and outs of it. We knew when the harvest had been good, or when it had been disastrous, and I suppose that's what put me off. I couldn't give my all to something that relied on the vagaries of the weather or could be destroyed by a disease of some sort. I like to know where I stand.'

Tom nodded agreement. 'I feel much the same way. I suppose we both take after our mother. She was always the practical one, the one who wanted to do something other than work a vineyard...but it was Dad's dream, and so she went along with him.'

Natasha smiled. 'Yes. Do you remember the time when she'd planned a day out and Dad didn't want to leave because he wanted to go out and inspect the crops?'

Their conversation faded into the distance. Katie found it hard to take in this glimpse of family life. It seemed strange to hear them talk about their relationships, the way that they had been at odds with their father. And yet they had loved him, there was no doubting it. That was what her father had denied her for so long. And now Nick was also to blame.

CHAPTER EIGHT

THE hotel's Garden Room was aptly named. Patio doors opened up onto a terrace, enlivened with stone tubs that were filled with bright, trailing begonias in shades of scarlet and yellow. Beyond that was a lawned area, bordered by trees and shrubs, with trellised archways and rustic fences providing support for scrambling clematis in various hues of pink and lilac.

The room was comfortably furnished with soft-cushioned sofas and low, glass-topped occasional tables. It was the perfect setting for a family meeting, but the atmosphere was tense, and Katie was feeling distinctly uncomfortable.

'I can't believe you're doing this.' A faint scowl marred Tom's features as he turned on Katie. 'You're acting on a whim, and your idea of holding onto the vineyard is going to ruin me. My business is failing and selling the vineyard is my way out. It would be different if we could sell our individual assets, but we can't, according to the will. It's all or nothing.'

'And I'm in arrears with my rent,' Natasha put in, 'and there are so many bills to pay I hardly dare open the envelopes when they come through the door. I even tried asking my ex for help, but he's struggling, too.' She hesitated, her gaze clouding momentarily. 'But, then, that's half the reason we split up. He couldn't make a go of his business and the strain was too much for us.'

'I can see why you're both upset,' Katie answered cautiously, 'and it's true I've only just come to know about the vineyard and all it represents...but it has been long enough for me to realize that it's very important to me.' She tilted her chin. 'You're forgetting that Jack was my father, too. I was his firstborn, and that means something to me. It means that I have his genes, and now I have a heritage that I want to safeguard. I'm sorry if that causes problems for you, but it's the way I feel.'

They stared at her in stunned silence, their expressions totally hostile. She didn't want to be at odds with either of them, and a surge of guilt ran through her, but with every fibre of her being she felt she had to stick to her guns.

She had been battling with them for the last hour and at times the argument had been heated and bitter. It left her feeling shaky inside, and it hurt that they had turned on her in such a savage way. It was easy enough to understand how they felt, but this was a once-in-a-lifetime opportunity and everything in her told her that she didn't want to let it go.

Was it selfish of her to want to carry on what her father had started? He might not have been the greatest father in the world. He'd let her down, but the vineyard was his handiwork, something to be proud of, the one solid achievement that she could preserve for posterity.

Her pager began to bleep. She checked the text message and said flatly, 'I have to go. There's been a road traffic accident.' She glanced at her half-brother and -sister. 'I'm sorry…perhaps Antony can help you to come to some arrangement over finances that will help you both out…but I've made my decision. Believe me, it wasn't an easy one…but I've been thinking about it for these last few weeks and I've made up my mind. I'm not prepared to sell.'

She left the room and hurried along to the hotel foyer, but she was taken aback to see Nick standing by the reception desk. He was talking to the manageress, looking through a brochure with her, but as Katie approached he turned away from the desk and let his glance drift over her.

Katie felt her stomach clench. She had been right to push him away, hadn't she? For all his careful attention and sweet-talking ways, he had shown that he was just like everyone else.

And what would he make of her dispute with her brother and sister? Most likely he would side with them and encourage them to pressurise her into selling. It would be in his interests to do that, wouldn't it?

'You're leaving already?' Nick said with a frown. 'I'd expected the meeting to go on for much longer.'

'I have to go out on an emergency.' Her voice was terse. 'There's been an accident on the main highway, with several cars involved, and they're calling for medics to attend.'

Nick's brows drew together, and as he handed the brochure to the manageress his phone began to bleep, signalling a text message. He quickly scanned it and then said, 'Me, too. It must be a bad one.' He turned to the woman once more. 'I have to go,' he murmured. 'Change the layout as we discussed and I'll look over the copy as soon as soon as you have it.'

She nodded. 'That's fine. You go ahead. I'll deal with this.'

'We should go,' Nick said, taking Katie by the arm. 'I can give you a lift—there's no sense in taking two cars, is there?'

'I suppose not.' Katie shrugged. 'I'll get my medical kit from the boot of my car.'

They set off just a few minutes later, driving along the main road from the hotel towards the coastal highway. Katie watched the rolling hills pass by, took in the magnificent cypress trees forming silhouettes against the skyline, and tried not to think about the fact that she was in Nick's car, that her heart was encased in ice, or that her siblings hated her.

'You're very quiet,' Nick said, turning the car on to the highway. 'How were things back there?'

'Not too good. Natasha was a bit edgy—she's worried about her little girl. She said she's tired all the while, but the doctor thinks the child's just a bit run down and it will pass.'

She frowned. From her experience she knew that doctors ought never to ignore a mother's instinct. But the toddler's symptoms were vague, and you could hardly expect the physician to be too worried at this stage. 'Tom seems to think the little girl is a fussy eater, and that might have led to her problems.'

'He could be right,' Nick murmured. 'At least the doctor's given her a check-up.'

'I suppose so.'

'So, how did the meeting go? You seem quite subdued. Was it not as you expected? It's a shame that you didn't get to finish it.'

'Perhaps it's just as well we were interrupted,' she

answered with a faint sigh. 'Things weren't going too
well. Tom and Natasha are very upset with me, and
I'm sad about that because I want to get on well with
them.'

He sent her a sideways glance. 'Why would they be
upset with you? You only had to talk over what you were
going to do about the estate, didn't you? I would have
thought that was a positive thing, albeit tinged with a
good deal of sadness. It's not every day you get to decide
how to manage an inheritance like that.'

'Well, there's the rub.' She made a face. 'We couldn't
agree on how to deal with it.'

He frowned. 'You'll have to explain. I've no idea
what could have gone wrong. I know they were very
keen on selling to my father and me. It was agreed that
Toby would stay on as manager, so there shouldn't be
any hitches.'

'No, there shouldn't…but you see, even you believe
it's all a foregone conclusion. Except that isn't how it is
at all.' She shot him a quick glance. He must have been
feeling very satisfied, thinking all was going to plan.

The thought depressed her. How could she have had
him so wrong? She had fallen for him, been caught up
in a whirlwind of emotion that had threatened to over-
whelm her, and life had become bright with the intense
colours seen through the eyes of new love. But it had
all faded, and she'd realised that she didn't know him
at all.

'Katie?' His quiet voice jerked her out of her
reverie.

'I told them I don't want to sell.'

His eyes widened. 'Are you quite sure you know what
you're doing?' he asked, his tone incredulous. 'How on

earth are you going to handle things? You have absolutely no experience of running a vineyard.'

'Then I'll have to learn, won't I?'

'Do you think it's just a matter of harvesting the crop and sitting back while the money rolls in?' He shook his head. 'It doesn't happen that way, Katie. It takes a lot of hard work and dedication.'

Her eyes narrowed on him. 'Do you think I'm not capable of that?'

His mouth twisted. 'That's not what I'm saying. I'm just pointing out that if you go ahead with this, it's quite possible you'll come a cropper.'

'And there wouldn't be just a hint of sour grapes in your reaction, would there?' she challenged him. 'I know how much you wanted the vineyard for yourself.'

'For my family.' The correction was brusque and to the point. 'Yes, we want it.' His eyes darkened. 'And I'm not giving up on that. The offer still stands.'

Her gaze was troubled. 'But I'm not going to accept it. Okay, I'm not at all sure I'm doing the right thing, and I really don't want to upset my family. I know they're going through a difficult time. But instinct tells me I shouldn't be making such a big decision about selling so soon after my father's death. If I let the vineyard go now, I might come to regret it some months or years down the line. I'm really keen on the idea of owning a stretch of land—my father's land—that produces some of the finest wines in California. For me, that's far more important than the money.'

'It's a huge undertaking. I think you're making a big mistake.'

'I know.' She frowned. Clearly, she was on her own in this, and if things went wrong, she would only have herself to blame. He was right. What did she know about owning a vineyard? The enormity of what she was planning to do began to crowd in on her, overwhelming her with all sorts of dire possibilities, and to distract herself she looked out of the window and gave her attention to the road once more.

They were passing through scenic countryside right now, and she could see the ocean in the near distance and she watched as waves crashed on to the rocky shore. It seemed to perfectly echo the way she was feeling right now.

A minute or so later they reached the point in the road where the accident had happened. Police officers had sealed off the area and set up diversionary routes for other drivers.

Katie looked around and then let out a slow breath. 'This is a mess,' she said softly.

Nick's mouth made a grim line. 'It looks as though an SUV turned over. From the skid marks, I'd say he tried to avoid something up ahead and everyone else piled in. You're right, it's a mess.'

'There are a couple of drivers in the cars who look to be in a bad way,' a police officer told them as they went over to the cordoned-off area and introduced themselves. 'The fire department is working to free them right now. We've led the walking wounded away to a place of safety, but there are two women in the SUV who look as though they have serious injuries. Seems the driver had to slam on the brakes when someone pulled out in front of her. She swerved and lost control of the vehicle and then ended up on the embankment at the side of the road. There are some others who are injured, but the paramedics don't seem to be too worried about them at the moment.'

'Thanks for letting us know,' Nick said. 'We'll go and check them out.'

Two ambulances were already on the scene, and the paramedics were doing triage, trying to find out which people needed attention first.

'Glad to have you along, Doc.' The lead paramedic nodded towards Nick and then gave Katie a brief acknowledgement. The two men obviously knew one another.

'The drivers of the cars have fractures of the legs and arms,' he said. 'They're in a lot of pain and discomfort, but we're doing what we can to stabilise them right now. It's the women in the SUV who need looking at. I think one of them is going into shock. My colleague did an initial assessment and we're giving them oxygen.'

'Okay, we'll see to them.'

Nick and Kate hurried over to the SUV. It was partially on its side, having come to rest on the embankment, but at least both women were accessible, albeit with some difficulty. Katie manoeuvred herself into the doorway of the vehicle and assessed the woman in the passenger seat, while Nick attended to the driver.

'Can you tell me your name?' she asked. The woman appeared to be in her early forties, and her companion was of a similar age, she guessed.

'Frances…Frances Delaney.' She struggled to get the words out, and Katie could see that she was having trouble with her breathing.

'Okay, Frances,' she murmured. 'I'm Dr Logan and I'm here to help you. Can you tell me where it hurts?'

'My chest. It's a bad pain.' The woman tried to point

to her upper rib cage, but then she tried to look round and became agitated. 'What's happening to Maria…to my sister?' she asked. 'She's not speaking—is she all right?'

Katie glanced to where Nick was carefully examining the driver. 'She's conscious,' she told Frances. 'Dr Bellini is looking after her.'

'She's hypotensive,' Nick murmured, 'and her heart rate is low. There's a contusion where the steering-wheel must have impacted, so I think we're looking at some kind of abdominal injury.' He looked at his patient. 'As soon as I've finished examining you, Maria, I'll give you something for the pain.'

Maria tried to say something, but couldn't get the words out. Katie's strong guess was that she might be asking for Frances, but the sound was indistinct and faded on her lips. 'Try not to worry, we're going to take good care of you and your sister,' Nick told her. He must have come to the same conclusion as Katie.

He had a soothing way with his patients, Katie reflected. He was gentle and soft spoken, and at the same time very thorough and methodical. Maria was in excellent hands.

She went on with her own examination of Frances. 'It looks as though you have some broken ribs,' she said quietly. 'And as far as I can tell, your forearm is fractured in two places. I'll give you an injection for the pain and immobilise it with a sling, but you're going to need surgery to fix the bones in place.'

Frances was white-faced and it was fairly obvious that her condition was deteriorating by the minute…something that started alarm bells ringing in Katie's head.

'Yes. Thank you for helping me.' The taut lines of

the woman's expression relaxed a little as Katie administered the injection. 'It's my sister I'm worried about,' she said, her voice husky with emotion. 'She's always looked out for me...we look out for each other. I can't bear the thought that...' her voice began to fail '...that something might happen to her.'

'Try not to fret yourself.' Katie frowned. Despite the nature of the arm injuries, it was the rib fractures that concerned her most. Her patient was already experiencing severe pain and breathlessness. As a doctor, Katie knew that first and second rib fractures were often associated with damage to important blood vessels, and if that was happening, time was fast running out. It was imperative that Frances be taken to hospital as soon as possible.

She set up an intravenous line so that she could give her patient fluids, a first stage in defence against shock and blood-pressure problems that stemmed from traumatic injury. Nick was doing the same for Maria, but his expression was serious, and she guessed he was concerned for his patient.

'How is she doing?' Frances whispered the words, straining to summon the energy from a well that was beginning to run dry. 'I can't hear her. I need...to know... she's all right.'

Nick's gaze met Katie's. He made a small shake of his head. Maria had lapsed into unconsciousness and he had secured an artificial airway in place in her throat.

'We're doing everything we can for her,' Katie said softly. 'We'll be taking her to hospital with you, just as soon as we can.'

Nick called for the paramedics to assist with spinal boards for both women, and within a matter of minutes they had stabilised the sisters sufficiently so that they could be transferred to the ambulance.

Katie went to check on the other injured people. She checked vital signs and applied dressings to stem bleeding where necessary, and when she looked around some time later, she saw that Nick was doing the same.

The injured drivers had finally been freed from their cars, and were at that moment being taken into the second ambulance.

As soon as he was certain everyone was secure, Nick started to gather together his medical kit. 'I want to follow them to the hospital and oversee things from there,' he told Katie. 'Is that all right with you? Otherwise I could arrange for someone from the hotel to come and pick you up.'

'No, it's okay. I want to go with you.' She walked with him to his car. 'I'm worried about both of them. I want to make sure that Frances has an angiogram—I'm pretty sure there's some internal bleeding, and if it isn't dealt with quickly she'll be in bad trouble.'

He nodded. 'Same here. Maria's heart rate is way too low, and her abdomen felt full and doughy when I examined her. I'm sure there's some bleeding into the abdominal cavity, and the problems with her lower rib cage make me think there could be damage to her liver or spleen. An ultrasound scan should tell us what's going on there. If we can't find where the bleeding is coming from, we'll have to do a peritoneal lavage…but whatever happens, we need to do it quickly.'

They set off, and Nick drove as fast as was possible towards the hospital, arriving there as the paramedics were unloading their patients from the ambulance.

Both he and Katie made their reports to the emergency

teams, and followed the women into the trauma room. 'Is Dr Wainwright on duty?' Nick asked as a nurse, Abby, hurried to assist.

She nodded.

'That's good.' He turned to Katie. 'He's the best vascular surgeon we have. If there's any damage to your patient's subclavian or innominate artery—or both— he's the man to put it right.'

'That's a relief.' A patient could die from an injury like that if it wasn't picked up in time, or if the surgeon was unable to stem the bleeding.

Nick was talking to the doctor in charge of the emergency room. 'I'd like to oversee my patient's ultrasound scan. I hope that's all right with you?'

'Of course. Any time. You don't need to ask, Nick.'

Katie went to discuss her patient's case with the doctor who was taking care of her, and a few minutes later she watched as Frances was whisked away to the angiography suite. The woman was agitated, distressed at having to leave her sister behind, and, unnacountably, as she saw the lift doors close on the trolley bed, Katie was overcome by a sudden tide of unhappiness.

Perhaps it had come about because this was the end of a long day. She had been hard at work in the paediatric unit this morning, before hurrying to the meeting with her half-brother and -sister, and now, in the aftermath of the traffic accident, she was beginning to register the dreadful impact of tending injured people in the wreckage of vehicles that had been slewn across the highway. She didn't know what had caused these feelings to well up inside her. She couldn't explain it, but her heart was heavy and she felt desperately sad.

'I need to go and get a breath of air,' she told Abby. 'I'll be outside in the courtyard if there's any news.'

'That's all right. I'll come and find you if there are any developments.'

'Thanks.'

Katie went out into the courtyard, a quiet, paved area where hospital staff could sit for a while on wooden benches set at intervals on the perimeter. There were a couple of cherry trees out there, along with tubs of velvet-petalled petunias that provided bright splashes of colour.

She sat down and tried to sort out the bewildering thoughts that were crowding in on her. She was feeling overwhelmed and off balance, and it scared her quite a bit because she wasn't used to feeling that way.

'Are you okay?' Nick came out into the courtyard a few minutes later and sat down on the bench beside her. He handed her a cup of coffee. 'Sorry it's a styrofoam cup—the coffee machine was closest to hand. I doubt you had time to enjoy the coffee and sandwiches I sent round earlier at the hotel...you seemed to come out of the room almost as soon as the waitress took them.'

'No, you're right, I didn't.' She frowned. 'Come to think of it, I haven't had anything to eat or drink since first thing this morning.' She sent him a quick look as she sipped the hot liquid. 'We had a few difficult cases to deal with in the paediatric unit this morning and I had to stay on for a couple of hours after my shift finished to make sure everything was sorted out properly.' She took another swallow of her drink. 'This is good...thanks.' Even the delectable aroma of the coffee teased her taste buds.

He smiled. 'Are you going to tell me what's wrong,

or do I have to prise it out of you? I know there's something, because you were very quiet back there and you had that far-away, hurting kind of look in your eyes.'

She hadn't realised that he'd been watching her. 'And there I thought your mind was all on your patient.' She cradled the cup in her hands and swallowed down the rest of the liquid.

He shook his head. 'You're the one who's always on my mind,' he said quietly. 'Everywhere I go. I think about you, wonder what you're doing or whether you're okay. And I know you're not okay right now, so you should tell me what it is that's bothering you. What's upset you?'

'I don't know,' she said simply. Did he really think about her all the time? She put the empty cup down on the floor. 'I watched Frances being wheeled away and this bleak feeling swept over me. She looked so devastated, so torn, because she was being separated from her sister.'

She looked up at him, her eyes troubled. 'Perhaps that was it. She and her sister seem to be so close to one another, and maybe I wish things could have been like that for me. I never had any siblings until now, and it was all I ever wanted, to share that family feeling with people close to me. Finding out about Tom and Natasha was a shock, but once I got used to the idea I realised that a whole new world had opened up for me. And then I went and ruined it by throwing a spanner in the works. I don't think they'll ever forgive me.'

'But you have to be true to yourself in the end, don't you? And that means sticking by your decision.' He put an arm around her and drew her close and she didn't have it in her to pull away from him. The truth was, she missed that closeness, that feeling of being cherished. A lump formed in her throat. 'Isn't that what your father would have wanted?' Nick asked. 'Either way you choose, you risk losing out in some way.'

'Maybe.' Her eyes clouded. 'I suppose you were just pointing out what I already know when you said I haven't a clue about running a vineyard. And that's perfectly true. Perhaps the enormity of what I'm taking on is just beginning to sink in. It's one thing to do it when you have back-up, but quite another when everyone who matters is against you.'

'And I'm included in that group, aren't I?' His mouth made a crooked shape. 'I don't want to cause you any hurt, Katie…but the vineyard is my heritage, mine and my brother's. Running the family business is in our blood, it flows through our veins as though it's part of our being. You're just beginning to feel something of that with this inheritance from your father.'

'And I'm finding just the thought of it a little overwhelming, as you said I would. But I can't turn my back on it. I just need to find the strength, from somewhere, to go on.'

She pressed her lips together. 'I've had to come to terms all over again with the kind of man my father was. I was hurt when I found he had another family who had been kept from me, and perhaps I overreacted.' She gazed up at him. 'It was like a betrayal, and I thought I'd done with all that. I thought I had this tough outer shell that couldn't be broken, but it wasn't so. I crumbled at the first blow. I'm every bit as weak as he was. I can't even hold it together in the emergency room.'

'You know that isn't true, Katie.' He wrapped both arms around her and folded her to him. 'You're forgetting that you've only just lost your father in these past few weeks. You can't make decisions—any kind of decisions—when you're still grieving. And you *are* grieving, even though you feel he let you down.'

His lips lightly brushed her temple and Katie realised that more than anything she wanted to nestle against him and accept the comfort he offered. 'You'd grown to love him,' he murmured. 'That's why you want to hold on to what he left behind. You see his touch in every row of vines, in every grape that ripens. That's how I feel, too, when I think about how my ancestors carved out this valley and planted their crops. We can't let it go, Katie. We're no different from one another, you and I.'

'Aren't we?' She gazed up at him, her features troubled. 'You seem to be so confident, in everything you do. I'm still struggling to find my way.'

'Then let me help you,' he said softly, bending his head to gently trace her lips with his own. 'Let me help you to forget your worries for a while.'

He kissed her again, a lingering, wonderful kiss that filled her with aching need and made her want to run her hands through the silk of his hair. She ought to have been wary of him, because she knew that he would never stop trying to make her change her mind and relinquish her inheritance. Wasn't that what he'd meant when he'd said it was the wrong time to be making decisions?

She was at war with herself. On the one hand she felt he had the power to destroy everything that mattered to her...what was there to stop him from piling on the pressure until she gave in and sold out to him? And on the other, she wanted to drink him in, as though he was the water of life, a fount of everything that could save her from herself and make her whole again.

But the moment was short-lived. He eased back from her, reluctantly dragging his mouth from hers, and she stared at him, her senses befuddled, until she gradually began to realise that she could hear the rustle of someone approaching.

'I thought you'd like to know that your patient is back from her angiography,' the nurse said. 'Mr Wainright is going to operate. And the other lady is in a bad way, too, by the looks of things. They've called for someone from the surgical team to come and look at her.'

'Thanks, Abby,' Katie managed in a low voice. 'I'll come back in and take a look at the films.' Reality began to set in once more. She felt as though she'd had a near miss…a brush with danger…but she didn't think she'd come away unscathed. She felt as though the life was being sucked out of her.

Nick stooped to pick up her abandoned coffee cup then straightened and waited for her to come and stand beside him. 'Ready?' he said.

She nodded, but she wasn't ready at all. Far from it. After that kiss, she was more bewildered than ever.

CHAPTER NINE

THE doorbell pealed, and Katie checked her watch as she went out into the hallway. It was mid-afternoon and she wasn't expecting anyone—though there was always the slim chance that Tom or Natasha might drop by to talk things through with her. It would be a relief if they did. She desperately wanted to try to clear the air between them.

It was neither of them. Instead, she opened the door to discover that Nick was standing there, casually waiting, one hand planted flat against the wall as he gazed around the vestibule.

'Katie,' he said, straightening up. 'I'm glad I've found you at home.'

His gaze travelled over her and already her body was on full alert. He looked good, too good for her peace of mind, dressed in dark trousers that moulded his hips and thighs and emphasised the taut line of his stomach and a loose cotton shirt that sat easily on his broad shoulders.

She pulled the door open wider and waved him into the hallway. 'Come in,' she said. 'This is unexpected. Is everything all right? Is there a problem at the hospital?' She led the way to the living room and tried not to think about the way he'd held her just the day before or the way his kisses had melted the ice around her heart.

'It's nothing like that. Everything's fine. I just thought you might want an update on the Delaneys. I know you've been asking about them.'

She nodded. 'No one was very forthcoming. I know Frances had arterial grafts to repair her damaged blood vessels, and her forearm fracture was so bad that both bones had to be fixed with metal plates and screws. She was still in a fragile condition this morning when I rang. But no one seems to be able to give me much information on Maria.'

'I think that's because the situation was complicated,' Nick explained. 'Both her liver and spleen were lacerated, but the surgeon managed to repair the damage. The biggest problem was that while he was operating he discovered damage to the pancreas. He did what he could to preserve the organ, but it's touch and go from here on.'

Katie sucked in her breath. 'Poor Maria.' Pancreatic trauma was often not detected until it was too late. Sometimes, if it was a simple contusion, it could be cleaned up and drained, but in Maria's case it sounded as though the damage was extensive. All they could do now was wait and see what happened.

'Thanks for coming here and telling me,' she said. 'I was hoping you'd follow up on them and let me know how they were doing.'

His glance touched her, moving over her features in a lingering, thoughtful manner. 'That's one of the things I love so much about you…that you care about people. They're not just patients to you, but people with families and lives outside the hospital.' His mouth flattened.

'Of course, that can be a hazard in itself. Getting too involved isn't always a good thing—not if you want to feel easy in yourself.'

Katie's gaze met his briefly. There were things he loved about her? She looked away. She'd been through too much heartache to start hoping all over again... hadn't she? How many times was she going to get up on to her feet, only to have life knock her down again?

If Nick wondered what she was thinking, he made no mention of it. Instead, he cast an appreciative glance around the room, his gaze lingering on the shelves that decorated one wall. 'It looks as though you've picked up one or two pieces from the fine-art shops around here,' he murmured.

'Yes.' She pulled herself together. 'I wasn't able to bring much with me from England, so I thought it would be good to brighten up the apartment with a few colourful touches here and there.'

He nodded, and turned his attention to the glassware on display. 'I like these bowls...the etchings on the glass make me think of sea life, with all those fronds and water plants.'

'They're similar to some my mother has at home.' Her mouth made a straight line. 'She and my father brought quite a bit of glassware from Murano. She likes to collect special pieces, paperweights and so on.'

Nick's gaze flicked over her. 'Have you forgiven him yet?'

The breath left her lungs in a sudden rush. 'I don't know. Perhaps.' After all, she'd been living with her father's imperfections for some twenty years. In the end, maybe she simply had to accept that he'd had genuine feelings for her. He'd told her he was proud of her, and he'd taken the trouble to warn her against falling for Nick. Though that was probably a warning that had come too late. Wasn't she already living with the consequences?

'And me?'

Her gaze faltered. 'Where you're concerned, I just think it's safer if I try to keep my wits about me.'

His mouth twisted. 'There must be some way I can get back into your good books,' he said softly. 'Maybe I could drive you over to Jack's vineyard so that you could have another look at the place? I know you've been so busy lately that you haven't been able to go over there.'

'And you think when I do I'll perhaps decide that I've made the wrong decision about keeping it?'

He laughed. 'Well, maybe that, too.' His expression became thoughtful. 'Actually, I heard Natasha was thinking of going over there this afternoon, and I guessed it might be a good opportunity for you to talk to her again—to the manager, Toby, as well, of course. He's usually up at the house at this time of day.'

She hesitated. Why was he doing this? Was it really as he said, to try to win her over, or did he have an ulterior motive? Did he think that when she saw the vast extent of the place once more she would realise she had taken on too much?

'It sounds like a great idea,' she murmured. 'Though I don't know how Natasha is going to react to me. I'm not altogether sure that there's anything I can say to her that will put things right.'

'I wouldn't worry too much about that. At least you'll have made the effort.'

'I suppose so.' She sent him a quick glance. 'Won't I be putting you out, though?'

'Not at all. I've been meaning to see Toby about a planting programme we were talking about last month. Your father and he were thinking about trying a new variety of grape, and my father wants to try it out, too.'

'Okay, then.' She hesitated. 'Are we ready to go now? I'll fetch my jacket.'

The approach to her father's vineyard took them through a glorious green valley, with pine-clad hills that soon gave way to row upon row of vines. The fruit was lush, soft hued as it began to ripen, and Katie felt an overwhelming sense that all was right with the natural world as she gazed at the sun-dappled slopes. If only her own life could be so serene.

Toby was at the front of the house, talking to Natasha, when they arrived, but they both turned to look in their direction as Nick drove on to the forecourt.

Natasha was holding Sarah in her arms, but she set the infant down on the ground once Nick had parked the car. A black Labrador had been padding about, sniffing amongst the flower-beds, but he came to greet them, tail wagging, as they stepped out of the car.

'Hi, there, Benjy.' Nick patted the dog on the head and received a boisterous welcome in return, the Labrador's whole body moving in excited recognition. Then it was Katie's turn, and she gently stroked the dog, tickling him behind the ears.

She smiled at Natasha but received a blank stare in return. Toby, on the other hand, nodded to both of them.

'Hi, there,' he said. 'I wondered if you might drive over today.' He was a tall man in his early forties, with brown hair and a face that was bronzed from many hours spent out in the sun. 'My wife had to go out, but she made some oatmeal cookies before she left, so we can enjoy them with a pot of tea. I'll put the kettle on and we can sit outside on the patio for a while, if you like. Then I'll show you around.'

Satisfied he had made his presence known, the dog went to lie down at his feet, regarding them all in a slightly curious fashion, raising an eyelid every now and again in case he was missing something.

'Thanks,' Katie said. 'That sounds good. I wanted to talk to you for a while, about the vineyard and so on.'

His expression was serious. 'I thought you might.'

'We were just going to take a look around the house,' Natasha said, glancing at Nick. 'There are one or two maintenance problems that have cropped up—like a couple of broken fences and some roof tiles that need to be replaced. Toby said he didn't mind fixing them, but I think he probably has enough to do already.' She looked at Katie, her expression cool and vaguely antagonistic. 'I suppose the ball's in your court. You were keen to take this on, so I dare say we can leave the decisions to you. Tom and I never wanted the stress of running the business and everything associated with it.'

Katie pulled in a deep breath. 'If that's what you want, then of course I'll deal with everything that comes along. I'll keep you up to date with what's happening.' She was disappointed by her cool reception, but she could hardly have expected anything else in the circumstances. Natasha was still annoyed with her, from the looks of things, but there was no point in getting into a state about it, was there?

Sarah toddled over to Katie and stood, gazing up at

her. Her bright curls quivered and shone in the sunlight. 'Pwetty,' she said, and for a moment or two Katie was taken aback, until the little girl pointed to her necklace. 'Pwetty,' she said again, and Katie smiled.

'You like it? It is pretty, isn't it?' She fingered the silver filigree necklace and crouched down so that the infant could take a better look. 'My mother gave it to me, so it's very special.'

'Best not let Sarah get her fingers round it, then,' Natasha said flatly. 'She doesn't distinguish between special or worthless. She grabs everything. One tug and it's ruined.'

'Oh, dear. Well, I'd best protect it, then, hadn't I?' Katie placed her fingers over the necklace and glanced towards Nick, wondering what she could do to distract the child.

'You can play with my keys for a while, if you like, Sarah,' he said, coming to the rescue by jangling them temptingly in front of the child's face. Her eyes widened and she turned her attention to Nick, the pink tip of her tongue coming out to touch her bottom lip as she gazed up at him. The keys were irresistible, it seemed, and she held up her hands, trying to grasp them as he gently teased her, darting them about in a catch-me-if-you-can kind of game.

It didn't have quite the effect he was looking for, though, because being thwarted proved altogether too much for her, and the toddler burst into tears.

Nick's jaw dropped, and Katie looked on in consternation. 'I was just playing with her,' Nick said. 'I didn't mean to upset her.' He turned to Natasha. 'Do you think she'll let me pick her up and comfort her?'

'You can try,' Natasha said. 'It isn't your fault, mind.

She's been like this for some time now, fretful and tear-ful, on and off. I just haven't been able to work out what's wrong with her. I've put it down to tiredness. She's been sleeping an awful lot lately, so perhaps the doctor was right when he said she was run down. I've just been letting her rest as and when she needs it.'

Nick picked up the little girl and cradled her in his arms, offering her the keys, but by now she had lost interest in them. She sobbed, large hiccuping sobs that racked her body, and tears trickled down her face, giving her a woeful expression.

'I'm sorry, cherub,' Nick said in a soothing tone. 'I was only teasing. I didn't mean to upset you.' He was thoughtful for a moment or two, and then asked quietly, 'How about I give you a rock-a-bye swing—would you like that, hmm?' He began to rock her gently to and fro in his arms, and after a while she stopped crying and stared up at him, her face pale.

Katie watched him with the little girl and felt a pang of emotion well up inside her. He was so natural with her, so caring and gentle, so obviously concerned for her well-being.

'You definitely have the knack,' Toby said with a laugh. 'I expect Natasha will be calling on you for babysitting duties from now on.'

'Heaven forbid!' Nick looked aghast. 'I'd need a bit more practice before I took up that kind of challenge.' He looked at Katie, a questioning, odd kind of look, and an unbidden thrill of expectation ran through her. What would it be like to have his children?

Toby showed them the way through the house to the kitchen, the dog following at his heels. It was a large breakfast kitchen with glass doors to one side leading out on to a terrace. 'Make yourselves at home out there,' Toby said, waving them out towards a teak wood table and chairs. 'I'll make the tea and bring it out to you.'

Nick was still holding his precious bundle, but now he looked over at Natasha. 'Do you want to take her?' he asked. 'She looks as though she's settled now.'

'Okay. I'll put her in her buggy,' Natasha murmured. 'She can sit and watch us while we talk.'

Katie glanced at the child as she lay back in her buggy a short time later. She was white faced, her curls slightly damp against her forehead as though she was a little feverish. Her breathing was rapid, and it occurred to her that the child looked exhausted.

Toby arrived with the tea, and once he had seated himself and they had chatted for a while, Katie brought up the subject of the management of the vineyard.

'I hope you'll stay on here and run things for us as you've always done,' she said. 'I know how much my father valued your work here.'

'Thank you. I'd like that.' Toby looked relieved. 'Does that mean my family can go on living here at the house?'

'Of course. I've asked Antony to draw up the paperwork to give you a more secure tenancy.'

Natasha sent her a quick look, but said nothing, and Katie said evenly, 'I'm assuming that will be all right with you and Tom?'

Her sister nodded, and soon after that Nick began to talk to Toby about the new planting programme. Benjy, who had been supposedly dozing at Toby's feet, was disturbed by a butterfly and decided he needed to go and check things out. As the butterfly flitted away to the flower border, he got to his feet and went after it.

'Up, Mummy!' Sarah suddenly exclaimed, looking at Natasha. 'Up.' She stretched out her arms to her mother, and Natasha frowned.

'If I lift you up, what then?' she said, giving her daughter a quizzical look. 'You'll be demanding to be set down, then, won't you?' She frowned. 'You want to play with Benjy, don't you?'

Sarah's expression was gleeful. 'Up...play Benjy,' she said, and by now her fingers were doing their familiar clasping and unclasping as if she was clutching at the air.

'Okay, then, young madam,' Natasha murmured, lifting the child out of the buggy. 'But try and stay out of trouble. No pulling at the flowers.'

'F'owers,' Sarah echoed happily. 'Benjy f'owers.'

Benjy was indeed exploring the flowers, Katie noticed. His nose was pressed up against them as he drank deeply of their scent, and a moment later he drew his head back and gave an enormous sneeze. Sarah giggled.

The dog's nose was covered with pollen, and Katie smiled. She looked at Nick and saw that he was chuckling, too. Their glances met in a shared moment of amusement.

Sarah toddled off to where Benjy was getting ready for another sneeze. She patted him vigorously in sympathy and then wandered away to inspect the scarlet begonias.

Katie watched her go, and saw how the little girl seemed to slow down and come to a standstill. It seemed that she had stopped to look at a ladybird or some such, but there was something about the way she was standing that had Katie's instincts on alert all of a sudden. Then the child's legs seemed to crumple under her and in an instant Katie was out of her seat. She hurried over to her, catching her as she would have fallen.

'What's wrong with her? What's happened?' Natasha was beside herself with worry. She rushed over and began to stroke her little girl's hair as though by touch alone she would bring her back to normal.

'She just collapsed,' Katie said softly. She used the second hand on her watch to carefully check the infant's pulse. Then she glanced at Nick, who had come to kneel down beside her. 'Her heart rate is very fast, and she's much too pale. I think perhaps she ought to have a proper check-up at the hospital.'

He nodded. 'I agree with you.' The dog came to find out what was going on, and Nick said softly, 'We should take her into the house.' He glanced at Natasha and she nodded.

'You could lay her down on the sofa in the living room,' Toby suggested. 'It's cooler in there. Maybe she had a touch too much sun.'

'It's possible,' Katie said, gently handing the child over to Nick, who lifted her into his arms and carried her into the house. 'We'll give her a few minutes to see if she comes round, but I think it's something more than that.'

'You thought she was ill earlier, didn't you?' Natasha glanced sharply at Katie as they gathered in the living room a moment or two later. 'I saw you looking at her when she was in her buggy.'

Katie nodded. 'If I'm right, I don't think it's anything too serious.'

'Tell me.' Natasha crouched down beside the sofa,

holding her child's hand, letting her know that she was there with her the whole time.

'Her main symptoms seem to be the tiredness and her pallor,' Katie murmured. 'You haven't mentioned anything else that's bothering you, apart from the fact that she's been quite fretful lately.'

'That's right.'

'And you mentioned some time ago that she had suffered from a viral infection—I'm guessing that this has been going on since then?'

'Yes… I think so.' Natasha's brows drew together. 'It's hard to know exactly when it started. It's been coming on gradually. What do you think is wrong with her?'

Sarah began to stir, rubbing her eyes and shifting to a more comfortable position.

Katie glanced at Nick. 'I'm thinking some kind of transient anaemia.'

'Yes.' He nodded. 'That sounds about right. Of course, we would need to confirm it with tests.'

'Anaemia?' Natasha's voice was filled with stress. 'Is that because of something I've been doing wrong? Haven't I been feeding her properly?'

Katie recognised the guilt in her voice. Parents often blamed themselves where no blame was due.

'No, it's nothing at all like that,' Nick said quietly. 'You don't often see this, but sometimes, after certain types of viral illness in young children, their bodies stop making red blood cells for a while. That would account for Sarah's tiredness and pale appearance.'

Natasha was horrified. 'That sounds awful,' she said. 'Can something be done? Is there a cure?'

He nodded. 'Usually it sorts itself out after two or three months.'

'But she collapsed. She can't go on like that, surely? That can't be right.'

Katie laid a hand gently on her arm. 'I know this is really worrying for you, Natasha, but Nick's right. Usually this type of illness clears up of its own accord. When a child collapses, though, as Sarah just did, it's best to get things checked out. She might need a transfusion. If this is what we think it is, that will help a lot and she'll soon start to feel better…though it's possible she'll need another transfusion before she recovers completely. At some point her bone marrow will start manufacturing the cells once more.'

Natasha had a panicked look about her. 'But I need to go and get help now. I want to take her to the emergency room.' She looked around distractedly. 'I shan't rest until I find out exactly what's happening.'

'I could take you to the hospital,' Toby offered, but Nick intervened.

'I'll go with her,' he said quietly. 'You stay and show Katie around the vineyard. I'm sure you must have a lot to talk about. Natasha and Sarah will be fine with me.'

'You don't mind?' Natasha asked. 'Are you sure? I don't mean to break things up, but I'm really worried about her.'

'Of course you are,' Nick said. 'I would have suggested it anyway. Sarah needs to be checked out.' He turned to look at Katie. 'Here, take my car keys. I'll take Natasha's car, and if we're delayed at the hospital for any reason, you can drive yourself home in mine. I'll pick it up later. Don't worry if you're not around when I come to collect it, I'll use my spare set of keys.'

'Okay.' Katie wasn't at all sure how she felt about driving his beautiful, streamlined car, but she judged that now wasn't the moment to dither or argue. It said a lot about him that he'd thought of her in this moment of crisis.

Natasha hurried away to gather together everything she needed to take with her while Nick secured Sarah in her car seat. The child was still drowsy, not really taking any notice of what was going on around her.

'Will she be all right?' Toby asked as he and Katie watched them drive away a few minutes later. 'I know you said it would clear up on its own, but it sounded pretty horrific to me. Anything to do with bone marrow not working properly is pretty scary, isn't it?'

'You're right,' Katie answered. 'Normally, it would be very worrying, but I'm hoping that this is one of those instances where she'll make a full recovery. We won't really know until we have the results of the tests.'

'It's a difficult situation—a worrying time all round.'

Katie nodded. 'Yes, it is.' She was glad Nick had gone with Natasha. He would be a comfort to her, and he would be able to explain anything that she didn't understand. He was a man to be relied on, a good man to have by your side in times of trouble. Or at any time, come to think of it.

She sighed inwardly. Her feelings for Nick were complex and very unsettling. Could it be that she was falling in love with him? In fact, the more she thought about it, the more certain she became that he was the one man who could make her happy...if only she could be sure that she could put her faith in him.

'Perhaps you'd like to look around the parts of vineyard you haven't already seen while we're waiting to hear what's happening?' Toby suggested. 'I know you were interested in the vines and the type of grapes that produce the Chardonnay. We have a separate area for the new planting on the west side.'

'Thanks. That would be great.'

The hills were bathed in sunshine at this time of day, and as they walked around, Katie was glad that she was wearing a simple, sleeveless cotton dress that kept her relatively cool and fresh. Even so, she was thankful for the occasional ocean breeze that fanned her hot cheeks.

Row upon row of glorious vines stretched out ahead of her, all of them in full leaf and heavy with fruit. 'You're doing a great job here, Toby,' she said.

'I do my best.' He sent her a quick look. 'These two vineyards, the Logans' and the Bellinis', have always been interconnected and run in a harmonious fashion. That might be under threat now that Tom and Natasha have shown that they're not interested.'

She frowned. 'You're afraid it will affect the smooth running of the place?'

'I think it might. At the moment they're happy for you to make the decisions, but that might not always be the case. There could be problems.'

She thought it over. 'I can see how that's a possibility—but right now I don't see any way round the situation. I can't afford to buy them out.'

'No.' Toby was quiet for a moment or two then added,

'I know Nick has an idea for smoothing things out. I expect he's spoken to you about it?'

She shook her head. 'No, he hasn't—except to say that he'd like to buy us out? Is that what he meant?'

Toby put up his hands as though to ward off any more questions. 'I'd better leave it to him to tell you his thoughts on that subject. Anyway, he wasn't specific, and I'm only concerned for the smooth operation of the vineyard.' He gave a wry smile. 'I don't want to get involved in sibling rivalry and multi-million-dollar takeovers.'

Katie stayed silent for a while after that. Toby's words had set up a welter of turbulent emotions inside her. Was Nick intending to increase his offer for the vineyard? How could he go on with his bid when he knew how much her father's legacy meant to her? She had begun to think he might have deep feelings for her, might actually come to love her, but now all her dreams were dashed once more. Her hopes had been reduced to ashes.

CHAPTER TEN

KATIE wandered barefoot along the beach, picking her way over craggy rocks and alternately feeling the warm sand glide between her toes.

There was so much to think about, so many questions that niggled at the back of her mind. What could Nick be planning? Would he really do anything to upset her? Why hadn't he rung to let her know what had happened at the hospital yesterday?

She missed him, she wanted to hear his voice, but instead there had just been a brief note pushed into her mailbox that morning to tell her that he had come along and collected his car while she was out—and to say that Sarah was being admitted to the paediatric ward so that the doctors could do tests. When Katie had tried to phone him, there had been no answer and the service had cut straight away to voice mail.

She stopped for a moment to listen to the calls of gulls overhead and to look around at the rugged, coastal bluffs. Out in the ocean, sea stacks rose majestically, carved out of ancient volcanic rock, a playground for sea otters that played offshore, feeding off the underwater kelp.

It was somehow soothing to be at one with nature…

but in the end it didn't take away her inner torment. How could it? Her life had changed so much in these last few months, and she'd had no choice but to confront her demons. Where had that left her? She was afraid and uncertain, full of doubt. And yet one thing shone clearly through the gloom—Nick had been a constant support to her, showing her how much he wanted her, gently coaxing her into loving him.

Just yesterday he had taken her to meet Natasha, and surely that was because he hoped they might somehow manage to heal the rift that had opened up between them. Would he have done all that if she meant nothing to him, if their relationship was just a spur-of-the-moment thing, a casual fling? She had to hope there was more. She couldn't go on this way.

For once, she had to take him at his word and trust in him. From now on she was going to meet life head on, which was why she walking along this stretch of sand, heading towards Nick's beach house.

Of course, she had rung Natasha. She had been desperate for news of her young niece, and at least her half-sister had recognised that she cared about the child and was worried about her.

'They're keeping her in overnight,' Natasha had said. 'It was late by the time the doctors worked out what they were going to do, but Nick was by my side all the while, explaining everything about the tests and so on. I don't know what I'd have done without him.' She pulled in a deep breath. 'Anyway, I'm going to stay here at the hospital so that I can be with Sarah. My husband—Greg—said he'd try to get here as soon as he can. He's been working away in the next county. We're both worried sick about her.'

'That's understandable,' Katie murmured. 'This must have come as quite a shock to you. I hope things turn out all right for you—will you let me know what happens?'

'Yes, I will.' Natasha hesitated. 'Thanks, Katie. I know you've been concerned for her all along and you were looking out for her. We've perhaps been hard on you, Tom and I. We both feel that we've misjudged you.'

'You've had a lot to deal with,' Katie said simply. 'You're my family. I just want to know that you're all doing well.'

It was a huge relief to know that they no longer bore her any ill-will, but the problems were still there. If she refused to sell the vineyard, they would go on struggling to keep their heads above water. What was Nick planning to do that would change all that? If things were to work out well for her half-brother and -sister, there could only be one loser.

She was overcome by doubts. If she was ever to make sense of any of this, she needed to see him, be with him…talk to him.

Katie pushed away a strand of chestnut hair that blew across her cheek in the faint breeze and walked closer to the water's edge. She paused to pick up a pebble and launch it into the ocean. It made a satisfying splash, and water droplets sprayed over her cotton dress. Waves lapped at her feet, cool, even after the heat of the day.

She halted for a moment, peering into the distance. From here she could just about make out Nick's house sheltered in the curve of the bay, and she set off once more towards it.

It was late afternoon, still warm, with the sun casting

its glow over all and sundry. Surely Nick would have finished his shift at the hospital by now?

It wasn't long before she reached the smooth stretch of sand that fronted his house, and straight away she saw that he was there. He was standing outside on the terrace, beneath the overhead deck, and he was facing her way. But he didn't see her because he wasn't alone and at this moment his companion was claiming all his attention.

A young woman was talking to him earnestly, her hand resting tenderly on his arm. Katie recognised her from her picture in the paper. This was Shannon, the woman he had once been engaged to, the girl he had supposedly abandoned.

Katie couldn't move. She stood and watched them, and after a second or two she saw Nick move closer to the girl and give her a hug.

The breath caught in Katie's lungs. She felt as though she had been winded, and she didn't know how to react. There was such a wealth of affection in that embrace, and it broke her heart. She stood transfixed, her pulse racing, a feeling of despair washing over her.

What was she doing, thinking that there might be a future for her with Nick? She was wishing on a moonbeam if she thought there was any chance he might have fallen for her. Hadn't Shannon always been there in the background? He'd made no secret of their relationship, had he? And in the end, hadn't he proved to be no different from her ex, professing to want Katie and at the same time making a play for someone else?

Slowly, her mind clouded by doubt and uncertainty, she started to turn away. She would talk to him later, when she had her head together a bit more. Seeing him with another woman was way more than she could bear right now. She loved him, and knowing that he was with someone else was just one more betrayal, perhaps the biggest betrayal of all because she had finally come to realise that he meant more to her than anyone in the whole world.

Her feet sank into the sand, slowing her down, but she made a huge effort to hurry away from there, even as she saw him glance in her direction and heard him call her name. She didn't look back but kept on going, putting as much distance as she could between her and the house.

'Katie…stop…let me talk to you.'

Still she kept on going. There was nothing to say, was there? She had made a mistake, and this was one from which she might never recover.

After a while he stopped calling after her, and even the silence was a rebuke. How could she have been so reckless as to fall for him? She meant nothing to him, did she? He had let her go without a fight. Perhaps he'd never wanted her in the first place, despite what he'd said.

She trudged on, oblivious to the call of the birds around her. She paid scant attention to the rare sight of brown pelicans nesting on the high bluffs or the black-headed terns that were searching for crustaceans among the rocks.

Minutes later, though, she stirred as she heard the drone of an engine in the distance. It was coming nearer, gaining steadily on her, the sound becoming louder and mingling with the crash of surf against the distant crags. She turned to see what was disturbing the peace and tranquillity of the bay.

'Nick!' Her eyes widened in astonishment as a dune buggy swung alongside her. 'What are you doing? Where did that come from?'

'It's mine. Hop in, I'll give you a ride along the beach.'

'No, thank you.' She shrank away from him. 'I don't think so. I really don't want to go anywhere with you.'

'Of course you do…you're just not thinking straight. Come on up here beside me.' The engine chugged to a slow, idling pace.

'I can't for the life of me think why I'd want to do that,' she muttered. 'I'd just as soon be on my own right now.' She frowned, looking the contraption over, studying the sturdy wheels and the open rails that allowed the warm air to move freely over its occupant. 'Anyway, I've never been in one of those things before. What's it for?'

He cut the engine. 'It's for catching up with headstrong young women who won't stop and take notice when they're called,' he said, reaching out a hand and grasping her by the wrist. 'Up you come. You'll like it… only hold onto the rail because the ride might get a bit bumpy around the rocks.'

She tried to resist, but his hold on her was firm and unyielding and after a while she realised that her struggles were fruitless and she may as well give in. There was no one around within shouting distance to come to her rescue, anyway.

Triumphant, he tugged her into the seat beside him. She glowered at him then settled herself more comfortably and brushed the sand off her feet before slipping on her sandals.

'Where are we going?' she asked as he started up the

engine once more. 'And what about Shannon—shouldn't you be with her? I saw you together. What happened? Have you just abandoned her? I'm sure she won't be very pleased to know that you're here with me.'

'Heaven forbid that I'd abandon her. No, she had to leave. She was only there on a quick visit—all she wanted was to let me know that she'd sorted out her problems.' He sent her a quick sideways glance. 'I thought we'd head along the beach to a nice, secluded spot...you never know when people are going to come along and disturb us on this section of the beach...and then you can tell me what's going on, why you came to see me and then turned away.'

'I decided what I had to say could wait until you were less busy,' she said in a pithy tone. 'It seemed to me that you had your hands full.'

'I thought that might be it.' The buggy gathered speed. 'You have a bee in your bonnet about Shannon, don't you?' he said, raising his voice to combat the sound of the engine. 'I keep telling you not to believe what you read in the papers. She's just a friend and she's been going through a bad time, but I guess you don't believe me, do you?'

Katie's mouth turned down at the corners. 'Perhaps it would help if you told me why she was at the hotel with you that night when the press caught up with you—and why, when I saw you with her just now, you had your arms around her?'

'Does that bother you?' He studied her thoughtfully for a moment and then turned his attention back to the beach ahead. 'Does it matter to you if I'm with someone else?'

'If it's another woman...yes, it matters.' She swallowed hard. There, it was out, she'd said it, something she'd hated to admit because it made her incredibly vulnerable.

'Good,' he said, in a satisfied tone, and she looked at him in shocked surprise. 'I hope that means you're jealous. I was beginning to think you'd never take me seriously.' He manoeuvred the buggy around an outcrop of rocks and steered it into a sheltered cove.

'I don't follow your reasoning,' she said awkwardly, looking at him wide-eyed. 'How can you care about me the way you say you do, if you're still seeing Shannon?'

His mouth flattened. 'Shannon is just a friend,' he said. 'I couldn't explain the situation before because she wanted to keep everything under wraps. The truth is, she's in love with someone her father doesn't approve of—he decided some time ago that he was a fortune hunter and did everything he could to break up the relationship. Of course, that was totally the wrong thing to do because it just encouraged them to have more clandestine meetings. Personally, I think the man she's chosen is okay. He cares about Shannon and wants the best for her.'

He parked the buggy by the foot of a cliff. 'Shannon was upset because her boyfriend was becoming wary of what her father might do—he'd threatened to cut her out of his life. So the boyfriend was thinking of going away because he didn't want her life to be ruined because of him. I was at the hotel that night when he'd tried to break it off with her, and she confided in me. We left the hotel separately, but the press had wind she was there and caught both of us on camera. They put two and two together and came up with five.'

'And now? After all, that was some time ago, wasn't it?' Katie looked at him doubtfully.

'Now she's trying to gain command of her life once more. She's made up her mind to go ahead and marry the man she fell in love with.' He gave a wry smile. 'To be honest, I don't think her father will cut her off. He loves her too much for that.'

'Oh, I see.' Katie's green eyes were troubled.

'I hope you do,' he said. 'But either way I'm glad you came to see me. Was there something special, or was it just because you couldn't stay away?' He grinned. 'I hope it was the last one.'

She pressed her lips together, still anxious. Even though he had put her mind at rest over Shannon, there was still a huge hurdle to face. She had to know what was on his mind when he spoke to Toby.

'I wanted to talk to you this morning,' she said, 'but I couldn't get through to your mobile.'

He nodded. 'I was swamped at work. We were inundated.'

'Yes, of course, I should have known.' She frowned. 'Is there any more news about Sarah?'

'They gave her a transfusion this morning and they're waiting to see if she perks up. From what the nurse said, she seems to be improving.' He paused for a moment. 'I think the doctors were worried about the cause of the anaemia initially, but now that the test results are back it appears it's as we thought. In time, she'll start to recover naturally. They say she just needs supportive care at the moment…rest, fresh air, a balanced diet.'

Katie let out a slow breath. 'That's good to know.'

'It is…and another snippet of good news is that I think Natasha and Greg will be getting back together.

They were always well suited—it was just that their money worries took over once Sarah came along. The fact that she's ill has brought them close to one another again.'

'I'm glad for them…and it's good to know that Sarah will have her father back with her.'

'Yes. It's always good when families are reunited. Which applies to the Delaneys, too, by the way. They moved Maria out of Intensive Care this afternoon. Apparently, her sister went to see her and they were able to talk for a while.'

'Oh, that's brilliant news.' Her face broke into a smile. 'That's been weighing on my mind for some time.'

'A lot of things seem to have been weighing you down lately.' He lifted a hand and gently stroked her face. 'Like this business of the vineyard. You're not happy about how it has affected Tom and Natasha, are you? I know things have been difficult between you.' His hand was warm against her cheek and she revelled in his comforting touch.

'It's worrying me,' she admitted. 'Though at least Tom and Natasha seem to have forgiven me. But I know they're going to have heavy burdens on their shoulders for some time to come, and I can't help feeling I might have done something to help them avoid that situation.'

'You still could.' He fingered the silky strands of her hair. 'If you let me help you.'

Her gaze meshed with his. 'Sell to you, you mean? I won't do that, Nick. I'm sorry. I made up my mind.'

'I know. I meant you could buy them out.'

She shook her head. 'How could I do that? I just don't have the means.'

'You could...' he paused to drop a kiss gently on her mouth, catching her off guard and setting off a flurry of warm sensation to fizz inside her '...if you'd allow me to lend you the money.'

She stared up at him, open-mouthed. 'But...but why would you want to do that?'

'Because I care about you.' He gazed down at the pink fullness of her lips. 'Because I want you to be happy. Because it's in my power to do it.'

Katie was shocked, thrown completely off balance by the enormity of his gesture. So this was his plan? To help her to keep the land that meant so much to his family? Words failed her, and her head was swimming with all kinds of thoughts, all of them leading to nowhere but utter confusion.

'I need to think about this,' she said huskily. 'I don't know why you're saying this to me. I never dreamed...'

She suddenly needed to escape the confines of the buggy. She slid down onto the sand and stared about her for a second or two, her mind in a daze. What he was suggesting was something she had never even contemplated...but why would he do such a thing?

He came to stand beside her, his arms folding her to him, his body close to hers, so close that it was all she could do not to cling to him and bask in the heady comfort of his warm embrace.

'What you're suggesting is incredibly generous,' she said huskily, her words muffled against the velvet column of his throat, 'but I don't see how I could accept. There's such a huge sum of money involved and I've no way of knowing if I could pay you back in the short or the long term. But thank you... I'm overwhelmed that you would even make the offer.'

The palm of his hand drifted lightly over the gentle curve of her spine, stroking her as though he would memorise every line, shifting to caress the rounded swell of her hip.

'You don't need to worry about any of that,' he murmured. 'It doesn't matter to me. All that matters is that you're happy and free from worry.' He gazed down at her. 'I don't know how it happened, Katie, but I've fallen for you big time. I'm completely out of my depth for the first time in my life and there's nothing I can do about it but accept it. I realised that some time ago. I love you... I need you... But most of all I want to make sure that you're safe and secure.'

The breath caught in her throat. 'I never imagined you would ever say that to me. I wanted it so much, but there was always this doubt at the back of my mind. I was scared. I'm still scared. I tried so hard not to love you because I was so sure I would be hurt...but it happened all the same, and now I'm...overwhelmed... elated...over the moon...' She closed her eyes briefly and absorbed the moment. 'I love you, Nick.'

He let out a ragged sigh and stooped to kiss her, exploring her lips with tender passion, sparking a trail of fire that flamed in every part of her being. 'Then nothing else matters,' he said softly, his voice rough edged as he came up for air. 'I'll always be here for you, Katie. You just have to learn to trust in me. I'll never hurt you, I promise you. You're part of me now. You've found your way into my heart, and we're bound together for all time.'

He darted kisses over her cheek, her throat, the bare

curve of her shoulder. 'Will you marry me, Katie? Please
say that you'll be my wife.' His expression was intent,
his eyes as dark as the ocean on a stormy day, and she
realised that he was holding his breath, waiting for her
answer.

'Yes... Oh, yes... I will,' she said in a soft whisper,
gazing up at him, her heart filled with joy. She reached
up to lightly stroke his face. She kissed him, running her
hands along his arms, his back, wanting him, desperate
to have him hold her closer, and he obliged, drawing her
against him, moulding his thighs to hers and pressuring
her into the safe haven of the cliff side.

'I want you so much,' he murmured, his voice husky
with emotion. 'I can't get enough of you, Katie. You're
everything I could ever want in a woman...so gentle,
thoughtful, so considerate of everyone around you.' His
mouth indented in a smile. 'When I saw you with young
Sarah, holding her in such a worried fashion, I thought
there was the woman I would want to be the mother of
my children. You're the only one for me, Katie. I love
you so much.'

She gave a sigh of contentment, her fingers roaming
lightly over his chest. 'I'd like to have your children
some day,' she murmured. Her gaze softened as she
looked up at him. 'Of course, if we should be lucky that
way, you know what it will mean, don't you?'

He shook his head and clasped her hand lightly, kissing her fingertips as though he would confirm his love
for her with each tender kiss. 'That we'll face the future
together as a family, come what may?'

'As a family,' she echoed. 'The Bellini family. And
the name will go on through the generations, just as you

wanted. Our vineyards would be linked under the same name as they were once before.'

'I hadn't thought of that,' he said. 'But, of course, it's true.' He smiled. 'It sounds like a perfect solution to me.' He wrapped his arms more firmly about her, and then he hugged her close and kissed her passionately, thoroughly, until her senses whirled and she was lost in a thrilling world of heady delight.

'I feel as though I've drunk too much wine,' she murmured contentedly. 'I feel as though my head is spinning and I'm so full up of happiness that I'm brimming over with it. Everything is turning out to be just perfect… you and me, and the solution to my brother and sister's worries. I never imagined things could turn out like this.'

'I'm glad you feel that way. I want to smooth out every glitch and make things perfect for you.' He laughed softly, running his hands over her as though to make sure she was really there, that he wasn't dreaming.

'I love you, Nick…only you. There's no other man I want in my life.'

He breathed a long sigh of relief. 'That's good. Because I really, really love you, Katie'

He bent his head and kissed her once more, and Katie clung to him and kissed him in return, loving him, loving the feel of him and wanting nothing more than to be with him for all time. For now she realised he was a man she could trust, a man who would be there for her always.It had taken her a long while to let down her guard, and finally she understood that he wasn't like other men. He would keep his promise to her, she could feel it in every part of her being, and she knew that she could look forward to a love that would last for ever.

She settled into his arms, kissing him tenderly, an ache of desire burning like a flame inside her. Why had she waited so long?

0111 Gen Std HB

MILLS & BOON®

FEBRUARY 2011 HARDBACK TITLES

ROMANCE

Flora's Defiance	Lynne Graham
The Reluctant Duke	Carole Mortimer
The Wedding Charade	Melanie Milburne
The Devil Wears Kolovsky	Carol Marinelli
His Unknown Heir	Chantelle Shaw
Princess From the Past	Caitlin Crews
The Inherited Bride	Maisey Yates
Interview with a Playboy	Kathryn Ross
Walk on the Wild Side	Natalie Anderson
Do Not Disturb	Anna Cleary
The Nanny and the CEO	Rebecca Winters
Crown Prince, Pregnant Bride!	Raye Morgan
Friends to Forever	Nikki Logan
Beauty and the Brooding Boss	Barbara Wallace
Three Weddings and a Baby	Fiona Harper
The Last Summer of Being Single	Nina Harrington
Single Dad's Triple Trouble	Fiona Lowe
Midwife, Mother…Italian's Wife	Fiona McArthur

HISTORICAL

Miss in a Man's World	Anne Ashley
Captain Corcoran's Hoyden Bride	Annie Burrows
His Counterfeit Condesa	Joanna Fulford
Rebellious Rake, Innocent Governess	Elizabeth Beacon

MEDICAL™

Cedar Bluff's Most Eligible Bachelor	Laura Iding
Doctor: Diamond in the Rough	Lucy Clark
Becoming Dr Bellini's Bride	Joanna Neil
St Piran's: Daredevil, Doctor…Dad!	Anne Fraser

0111 Gen Std LP

MILLS & BOON

FEBRUARY 2011 LARGE PRINT TITLES

ROMANCE

The Reluctant Surrender	Penny Jordan
Shameful Secret, Shotgun Wedding	Sharon Kendrick
The Virgin's Choice	Jennie Lucas
Scandal: Unclaimed Love-Child	Melanie Milburne
Accidentally Pregnant!	Rebecca Winters
Star-Crossed Sweethearts	Jackie Braun
A Miracle for His Secret Son	Barbara Hannay
Proud Rancher, Precious Bundle	Donna Alward

HISTORICAL

Lord Portman's Troublesome Wife	Mary Nichols
The Duke's Governess Bride	Miranda Jarrett
Conquered and Seduced	Lyn Randal
The Dark Viscount	Deborah Simmons

MEDICAL™

Wishing for a Miracle	Alison Roberts
The Marry-Me Wish	Alison Roberts
Prince Charming of Harley Street	Anne Fraser
The Heart Doctor and the Baby	Lynne Marshall
The Secret Doctor	Joanna Neil
The Doctor's Double Trouble	Lucy Clark

0211 Gen Std HB

MARCH 2011
HARDBACK TITLES

ROMANCE

A Stormy Spanish Summer	Penny Jordan
Taming the Last St Claire	Carole Mortimer
Not a Marrying Man	Miranda Lee
The Far Side of Paradise	Robyn Donald
Secrets of the Oasis	Abby Green
The Proud Wife	Kate Walker
The Heir From Nowhere	Trish Morey
One Desert Night	Maggie Cox
Her Not-So-Secret Diary	Anne Oliver
The Wedding Date	Ally Blake
The Baby Swap Miracle	Caroline Anderson
Honeymoon with the Rancher	Donna Alward
Expecting Royal Twins!	Melissa McClone
To Dance with a Prince	Cara Colter
Molly Cooper's Dream Date	Barbara Hannay
If the Red Slipper Fits...	Shirley Jump
The Man with the Locked Away Heart	Melanie Milburne
Socialite...or Nurse in a Million?	Molly Evans

HISTORICAL

More Than a Mistress	Ann Lethbridge
The Return of Lord Conistone	Lucy Ashford
Sir Ashley's Mettlesome Match	Mary Nichols
The Conqueror's Lady	Terri Brisbin

MEDICAL™

Summer Seaside Wedding	Abigail Gordon
Reunited: A Miracle Marriage	Judy Campbell
St Piran's: The Brooding Heart Surgeon	Alison Roberts
Playboy Doctor to Doting Dad	Sue MacKay

MARCH 2011
LARGE PRINT TITLES

ROMANCE

The Dutiful Wife	Penny Jordan
His Christmas Virgin	Carole Mortimer
Public Marriage, Private Secrets	Helen Bianchin
Forbidden or For Bedding?	Julia James
Christmas with her Boss	Marion Lennox
Firefighter's Doorstep Baby	Barbara McMahon
Daddy by Christmas	Patricia Thayer
Christmas Magic on the Mountain	Melissa McClone

HISTORICAL

Reawakening Miss Calverley	Sylvia Andrew
The Unmasking of a Lady	Emily May
Captured by the Warrior	Meriel Fuller
The Accidental Princess	Michelle Willingham

MEDICAL™

Dating the Millionaire Doctor	Marion Lennox
Alessandro and the Cheery Nanny	Amy Andrews
Valentino's Pregnancy Bombshell	Amy Andrews
A Knight for Nurse Hart	Laura Iding
A Nurse to Tame the Playboy	Maggie Kingsley
Village Midwife, Blushing Bride	Gill Sanderson

MR